From the Files of

Madison Finn

Read all the books about Madison Finn!

From the Files of
Madison Finn

Caught in the Web

By Laura Dower

HYPERION

New York

Text copyright © 2001 by Laura Dower

From the Files of Madison Finn, Volo, and the Volo colophon are trademarks of Disney Enterprises, Inc.

Printed in the United States of America

First Edition
7 9 10 8 6

The main body of text of this book is set in 13-point Frutiger Roman.

ISBN 0-7868-1556-6

Visit www.madisonfinn.com

For Rich and the monkeys

Special thanks to Karl
for teaching me how to use a PC

"So even though this guy was dead, his heart was still beating under the floor?" Hart Jones cried. "For real?"

"Well," Mr. Gibbons said. "Not exactly, Hart. But your imagination's working. That's good."

Madison Finn shifted in her chair. English class was giving her the creeps today.

Mr. Gibbons continued to pace in front of the class as he explained more meaning behind "The Tell-Tale Heart." He replayed a recording of the classic short story by Edgar Allan Poe.

. . . *The beating grew louder, louder! I thought the heart must burst.* . . .

This narrator's voice was weirder than weird.

. . . Until, at length, I found that noise was not *within my ears . . .*

"So his mind was playing tricks on him," Hart said aloud.

Mr. Gibbons clapped, excited. He liked it when his students gave good answers.

Hart always said things in class that made teachers smile. He was smarter than smart. This was probably why Madison had been crushing on him since seventh grade started. Plus, he was cute.

Way back in elementary school Hart had chased her around the school yard, but Madison always ignored him. Back then, Hart had been nothing more than a big geek. But something had changed over the years. His family moved away from their neighborhood in Far Hills. They moved back again when Hart was suddenly popular. Even Madison's enemy, Ivy Daly, appeared to have both eyes on him.

Fiona Waters leaned over to Madison. The beads on her braids clinked against the desk.

"Was Hart Jones just looking over *here*?" Fiona asked. "I swear I saw him. I swear."

"No way," Madison said firmly, turning in her chair. She shrugged off Fiona with a casual "Whatever." For a friend who was usually pretty spaced out, Fiona was paying an awful lot of attention to people Madison "liked" and "didn't like."

Hart had absolutely not glanced over in Madison's direction.

Had he? Now Madison wasn't sure.

Madison's lips were Ziploc-sealed shut when it came to boys. Only her secret computer files and her secret online friend Bigwheels knew the whole truth about her feelings for Hart and everything else.

Across the classroom, Ivy's hand shot into the air. She looked like a boa constrictor ready to strike. She had her elbows up on her desk and her red hair was all fluffed out around her head.

"Mr. Gibbons?" Poison Ivy hissed. "Can't you just tell us why the man killed the other man again?"

A kid from the back row laughed out loud. "Duh, weren't you listening?"

"Duh, yourself." Ivy turned around and glared. "I was so listening!"

"Excuse me." Mr. Gibbons clapped again because he wanted everyone to be quiet. He handed a spiky-haired girl in the front row a stack of papers. "I think we've talked about 'The Tell-Tale Heart' for long enough, class. Now, take one of these sheets and pass the rest along. . . ."

Madison saw the word *Boo!* in giant black letters on the page. A cluster of black bats winged across the top. Underneath, Mr. Gibbons had printed random facts about the origins of the upcoming holiday.

Much to Madison's surprise, the Halloween described on this paper had very little to do with the holiday she'd understood all her life. Centuries ago in Europe, Halloween was named "Samhain." Mr. Gibbons pronounced it "soh-wen." Samhain started out as a Celtic holiday.

"Wait! Wait! Who are the Celtics again?" Ivy asked aloud.

"Just one of the best basketball teams *ever*," Fiona's brother, Chet Waters, snapped.

Mr. Gibbons laughed. "You're right, Chet. But the real Celtics, or Celts, mentioned here were people from ancient Ireland. At the time we're talking about, in the fifth century B.C., Samhain, or Halloween, was the day their summer ended. On your sheet there's more information—and I added a crossword on the other side. . . ."

Madison loved word games. She flipped the page over instantly. This crossword was shaped like a witch's hat.

"Pssst! Maddie?" Fiona asked, leaning over toward Madison's desk. "Can you sleep over on Saturday? I'm going to ask Aimee too. My mom said it was okay."

"Cool!" Madison smiled. She loved sleepovers.

Madison timed herself filling in all the crossword puzzle blanks. Three minutes later, she'd scribbled the answer to each clue, finishing up just before the class bell. It was a personal record.

Fiona grabbed Madison's arm as they walked out.

"My mother says she'll make minipizzas and Cherry Garcia sundaes in honor of your favorite ice cream flavor," Fiona bubbled. "At the sleepover I mean. And my dorky brother, Chet, won't be there, so we can rent any old movie we want. I am soooo excited!"

Madison stopped short in front of a display case as they walked down the hall together. "Look," she said, motioning to Fiona. She pointed to a bright orange sign inside the cabinet:

Something to Scream About!
Halloween Dance
Friday, October 27, from 6 to 9 P.M.

"Yeah! Aren't you excited?" Fiona asked when she read the sign. "Seventh-grade dance committee meeting's tomorrow. We have to do the decorating and food and stuff like that."

Madison acted happy, but deep down, the dance had her a little worried. School dances usually meant a girl needed to be able to do three things: get boys to like her, pick out a cooler-than-cool outfit, and dance. Madison wasn't sure she could do *any* of those things.

She considered the possibility that maybe her luck was changing, however. Seventh grade was a new start, Madison told herself, so maybe all the tricks of the past would now turn into *treats*?

Madison headed over to Mrs. Wing's classroom to

help download some documents onto the school Web site. She'd been helping with the site since school started, usually after school and during free periods.

Staying after school could be a very good thing. Especially today. Madison knew Mom would be home late because of a meeting. Aimee had dance troupe. Fiona had soccer. If she stayed after school, Madison could avoid being alone so much. She'd get to walk home with her friends, after all.

On the way home, Aimee started chattering about the Halloween dance, but Fiona wanted to talk about sleepover plans exclusively. Madison asked Aimee if she could bring her mother's Ouija board.

"What's a wee-jee?" Fiona looked confused.

"You know, Fiona," Madison said. "You sit around in the dark and move this little pointer on the game and ask the ghosts to come and play. Like ooooooh, I'm so scared!"

"You shouldn't mock ghosts, Maddie," Aimee said. "Seriously."

"Aimee!" Madison groaned.

"There *are* ghosts everywhere," Aimee said with a straight face, pointing to an old building they passed on the route home. "Everywhere. You saw *The Sixth Sense*."

"There are *no* ghosts in Far Hills." Fiona shuddered. "Would you quit saying spooky stuff?"

"Yeah, Aim. I've had the jeebies all day," Madison said, thinking back to the story from English class.

"See? That's because you do believe me!" Aimee smirked.

As the sunlight faded, all the houses seemed soaked in an eerie, orange glow. While clouds and night sky gathered overhead, light played tricks on the sidewalk.

"You never know when there are ghosts around. They could be at school or anywhere. That's all I'm saying," Aimee said, hustling ahead of her friends.

Madison and Fiona looked at each other and then rushed to catch up. All Aimee's ghost talk *had* changed their minds a little. Suddenly every bush along the side of a dreary road was hiding a monster, every shadow on a deserted street was a beast on the loose, and every noise was the sound of heavy, plodding footsteps. . . .

Madison was so relieved to finally reach her front porch. She pulled her house key out of her bag. Phineas T. Finn, Madison's pug, greeted her with a big, wet, doggie smooch when she walked in the door. She couldn't hear anything at first except the dog's heavy breathing and snorting in her ears.

. . . Until, at length, I found that noise was not *within my ears. . . .*

Her mind wandered back to "The Tell-Tale Heart" again. Ghost stories at school and on the way home

7

were definitely *not* a good idea. Especially when she was home alone.

Madison called Mom's cell phone to check in. After getting the automatic voice mail system and not a real live Mom, she left a long message. Nerves made her ramble on a little bit longer than usual.

As she entered her bedroom, Madison flicked on the light and knelt down to look under the bed. But the only things Madison saw were a sock covered in dust, a notepad with Phin's chew marks, and one very dirty nickel.

Madison checked every closet and corner and crevice.

She even peeked behind the shower curtain in the hall bathroom.

What if there were ghosts in Far Hills?

Relieved when she found nothing resembling a ghost, Madison shook off her jeebies, slipped out of her sneakers, and sat down at her desk. She dialed her mom once again and got a busy signal this time. Mom was probably getting her messages. She'd be home soon, anyway.

Madison hadn't checked her laptop computer for e-mails yet today, so she powered it up. It was still sitting open on her bedroom desk exactly where she'd left it plugged in that morning. One click and the motor hummed again. After the home screen illuminated, Madison's e-mailbox flashed with a *ping*.

FROM	SUBJECT
✉ Bob1A1239	Invest NOW $$$

Who was Bob1A1239? His name looked like a real name, like a person from school. It annoyed Madison to think that someone was e-mailing her while pretending to be a regular guy. He wasn't real! She knew it must be an advertisement and immediately deleted the message. Dad always said to do that when she didn't know the sender.

FROM	SUBJECT
✉ Eggaway	Computer?
✉ Boop-Dee-Doop	Spooktacular SALE
✉ JeffFinn	FW: Ha Ha Halloween

Unlike Bob1A1239's message, the remaining notes in Madison's mailbox were from a more familiar crew.

Egg needed homework questions for Mrs. Wing's computer class.

Boop-Dee-Doop, an online clothes store for girls, was having a sale.

And Dad had sent along another one of his jokes. Madison always tried to guess the punch line.

What do you put on a Halloween sundae?

Whipped scream was the answer. She guessed it right away, but she still giggled. Dad's e-mails were like happy shots. It didn't even matter if she'd heard a joke before.

Madison opened a saved document and typed the sundae joke into her Dad file. It was joke number thirty-two so far this month. After that she went into her file marked "Social Studies." She'd created folders for every single subject with ongoing vocabulary lists. Tonight she had to study terms about archaeology. Her teacher, Ms. Belden, said she might be popping a pop quiz tomorrow.

Madison didn't want to take any chances.

By the time she memorized the definitions, it was already six o'clock. Her stomach was grumbling. Her e-mailbox *pinged* again.

FROM   SUBJECT
✉ Webmaster@bigfis   Are you CAUGHT IN THE

The new e-mail was an announcement from her favorite Web site, bigfishbowl.com. Text at the top flashed orange and white in honor of the season. The words looked like candy corns.

```
From: webmaster@bigfishbowl.com
To: Members Only
Subject: Are you CAUGHT IN THE WEB?
New Contest!
Date: Mon 16 Oct 11:50 AM
Are you caught in the WEB?
Well, get snagged NOW!

The big fins at bigfishbowl.com want
```

YOU to write us a mystery for Halloween. We provide the story starter and you provide the thrills! This is a special contest for bigfishbowl members ONLY.

Contest entries due Friday, October 27.

To enter the contest: Every winner MUST begin with the story starter below. Write a story of no more than five hundred words. The winner will have their mystery posted on our site and get a mystery game valued up to $25.

IT WAS A DARK AND STORMY NIGHT. THE HOUSE WAS DEAD QUIET, EXCEPT FOR . . .

"Dinner!"
Madison jumped. The message disappeared from the screen. Her pulse was racing so hard all of a sudden that she mouse-clicked the wrong icon on her computer screen.

"Whoa! Mom scared me," Madison said to Phin.

"Madison!" the downstairs voice bellowed again. "Sorry I'm late! Is Phinnie up there with you?"

"Yes!" Madison bellowed back.

"Rowrooooo!" Phinnie howled.

11

"Come downstairs!" Mom yelled again. "I got takeout, honey bear! Come and eat!"

Madison wasn't surprised about the menu. Mom had a habit of providing on-the-run dinners for the two of them. Madison usually categorized these meals as "Scary Dinners" in her computer files.

After inhaling the takeout Chinese vegetables and crunchy noodles, Madison started over-thinking.

She thought about the contest.

She thought about ghosts.

She thought about what she wanted for dessert.

"Penny for your thoughts," Mom said gently, reaching into a white, greasy bag. She produced a slice of cake in a pink plastic carton with frosting smudged on the side.

Had Mom eavesdropped on her mind? Madison contemplated the chocolate, double-butter-cream universe sitting on the table.

Mmmmmm.

She couldn't wait to take the first bite.

 Caught in the Web

Maybe if I could write scary stories,
I'd win this new Caught in the Web contest
on bigfishbowl. Can my writing possibly
compare to Edgar Allan Poe's "The Tell-Tale
Heart?"

I could write a "My Teacher Is Really
a Vampire" story. I'd write it about my
science teacher, Mr. Danehy, since he

really bites. But who would read
that?

Maybe I should just write about Ivy Daly
and Hart Jones dancing together at the
school dance. Now *that's* scarier than
scary.

Here's the truth: the only Halloween
story I'm gonna be able to write is "The
Tell-Tale *Hart*," without the *e* and without
me.

Rude Awakening: Life gets tricky around
Halloween.

Chapter 2

The Far Hills Halloween Dance Committee meeting was scheduled to begin at three o'clock on Tuesday, just after the last class bell rang. Madison was so excited about the meeting that she had a hard time focusing on her end-of-the-day social studies pop quiz.

She wasn't the only one. Aimee and Fiona were just as distracted. In fact, Fiona was doubly distracted because after the dance meeting she had soccer. It was the end of the season, and important games were coming up. She couldn't miss a single practice.

Fiona had considered skipping the dance committee altogether, but Madison convinced her to change her mind. The Halloween dance was *the* turning point at Far Hills. It meant that seventh graders could finally be a part of junior high. They were responsible for planning the important tasks like decorations, food, and music.

Aimee wasn't going to miss *any* of it. All four of her older brothers had gone to Far Hills Junior High.

Her oldest brother, Roger, told his sister the dance was an inauguration ceremony. "Like you're finally a member of junior high," Roger said. "Not just some visitor."

Her brother Dean, a high school senior, said the dance had been a great way to get noticed and to "meet babes."

Doug, the ninth grader who'd been to the dance only two years before, said the food was the best part. He hadn't actually *danced*, but he said the decorations "rocked."

Only Billy, Aimee's second-oldest brother, had voiced a negative opinion. He said the "dumb dance was so boring."

But he would say that. *Billy* was so boring.

Unfortunately, Aimee's brothers couldn't really help Madison figure out what she needed help with the most, like what outfit to wear or how to dance. More than anything, Madison wanted to dance with Hart.

Just as she thought about Hart, he walked into Señora Diaz's classroom. Madison nearly gasped out loud.

It was a sign. It was just like the night before

when she'd been thinking about eating dessert and Mom gave her chocolate cake.

"Hey, Finnster," Hart said, sliding into a seat in the front row. His hand grazed her shoulder accidentally as he walked by.

She felt her face get all red, so she tried to focus all of her energy onto a poster of Barcelona, Spain, that was hanging directly ahead of her on Señora Diaz's wall. It said PARADISE. She stared at the words until they got fuzzy.

Fiona whispered from behind. "Hey, Maddie, did you see that Web contest on bigfishbowl?"

Madison turned around. "Uh-huh. I'm gonna do it," Madison mumbled. She was happier than happy to get her mind off Hart. "Are you?"

Fiona shook her head.

"What are we talking about?" Aimee asked from one row over. "Are we talking about the dance?"

"No, *we're* talking about an Internet contest," Fiona said. "On bigfishbowl."

Out of the corner of her eye, Madison tried to watch Hart *and* talk to her friends at the same time, but it wasn't working so well. Hart was turned halfway toward them, wearing a jewel-green shirt that made his eyes sparkle. She still had a ghost of a feeling where his hand had brushed her arm.

"Earth to Maddie," Fiona joked.

"Oh. Sorry." Madison snapped back to the conversation. "Bigfishbowl. Yeah, the Web site, Aimee, where you can go online and chat. You know."

"I know *that*, Maddie." Aimee chuckled. "But I'm pretty much clueless about online chatting." Madison didn't understand how Aimee's dad could have a cybercafé in his bookstore, while Aimee still hadn't gotten her own screen name.

"But you are the queen of chatting, Aimee," Madison teased. "Just not on the computer."

"Which is why you just have to sign up!" Fiona commanded. "Then the three of us can meet up on bigfishbowl and talk. You can get your own screen name. It'll be the best, Aimee."

Fiona explained how she and her brother, Chet, had twin screen names. She was Wetwinz with a *z*, and her brother Chet was Wetwins with an *s*. Aimee agreed that was pretty inventive.

The classroom began to slowly fill up. Madison counted sixteen volunteers. Even Egg and his good buddy Drew were there.

Señora Diaz charged in behind students. *"Hola, estudiantes!"* she proclaimed, a little out of breath. *"Cómo están? Tienen ganas de que llegue el baile?"*

Most kids didn't have a clue about what was said since they were in beginners' French, not Spanish. But Egg tried to help. "She wants to know if we're excited about the dance," he explained.

If anyone could translate Señora Diaz, Egg could. Señora Diaz was his real-life mother.

"Thank you for your help, Walter," Señora said sweetly, as if she were pinching his cheek. Egg muttered something under his breath. Madison knew he hated it when Señora called him by his real first name like that. Mothers who were teachers were way more embarrassing than plain old ordinary mothers.

"Señora Diaz." Aimee's hand was up in the air. "Are we supposed to wear costumes to this dance?"

A kid in a blue jacket sitting near the door asked, "Do we have to pay?"

"Is there going to be stuff to eat?"

"Will there be a live band?"

"Settle down, everyone." Señora inhaled deeply and scratched her head with her pen. "Let's go slowly. *Estámos preocupados, no?* Lots of ground to cover."

A couple of kids groaned. Egg leaned across a desk and whispered, "What are *you* going to the dance as, Maddie? A dork?"

"Quit it," Madison growled.

"Silencio!" Señora said as she handed a piece of paper to someone in the front row. "Please pass this sheet around and sign up your names and homeroom and phone number. This is our committee contact sheet."

They would be splitting up into task teams for whatever needed to get done. Seventh graders had all the grunt work of the dance. Eighth and ninth graders just had to show up.

"Are we doing a scary hallway?" Aimee asked. "My brothers said we always do—and that it's the best part of the whole dance."

"*El Vestíbulo! Sí!* Of course!" Señora Diaz said. *Vestíbulo* was the Spanish word for "hallway." In addition to decorating the main part of the gymnasium with streamers and signs, designated areas of the gym would be set aside with aisles of space just wide enough for kids to pass through in the dark. Curtains were drawn all around that space to form a labyrinth. No one could tell which direction was which once inside the curtains. Plus students volunteered to "stand and scare" as unwitting visitors passed through.

"You scream as kids go by," Señora said. "*Un grito!* Right, Walter?"

Egg shrank down into his chair.

All Drew could do was snort. He always laughed when Egg got embarrassed. He laughed whenever Egg did *anything*.

Madison was busy deciding what task team she wanted to help with most. She knew she didn't want to scream in the scary hallway. She didn't want to deal with food, either. That was too messy.

Decorating seemed like the best option. She got along well with crepe paper, balloons, and masking tape. Madison had an eye for color, especially the deep orange of construction paper pumpkins.

Thwack!

The door slammed open and the entire room got as silent as a tomb. Everyone turned.

Ivy walked in fifteen minutes late. She said, "Sorry," but she didn't look very sorry. She flipped her hair twice. "This is the Dance Committee, yeah?"

"Take a seat, dear," Señora Diaz said, motioning down toward the front.

"Ex-cuse me," Ivy said, stepping over someone's bag. She made a big scene, stepping on four kids just to get to the one empty chair down near Señora's desk. It was the chair next to Hart.

Madison glared at the space between their seats. She imagined a force field or fence between them. One touch, and *pzzzzzzt!*

"Look who's here—" Aimee whispered, gently nudging Madison. "Figures."

By the time she got settled, Ivy's late entry had caused so much commotion that the meeting was temporarily off track. Egg and Drew were cracking each other up. One kid in the back row even had a Gameboy out.

"Atención!" Señora Diaz yelled. "Jacob, put that computer game away now or I'll confiscate it. Look, I think we need to make a dance committee rule that any latecomers to meetings will be excused—permanently—unless I get some valid note or explanation. Is that clear?"

Madison wished Señora would "permanently excuse" Ivy right then and there.

"Ahem." Ivy cleared her throat and spoke up in a soft voice that sounded nothing like the obnoxious Ivy Madison knew. "I'm really, really, *really* sorry about being late, Señora."

"Oh?" Señora Diaz crossed her arms. "And your note?"

"I don't have a *note* exactly, but I was at the nurse . . . and next time of course I'll get one. I am sooooo sorry."

"What a liar!" Madison thought. She knew for a fact that Ivy had been nowhere near the nurse that day. She wasn't *sick*! She'd probably been in the girls' bathroom, putting on lip gloss. Ivy sounded so sticky sweet, but Madison knew about the poison that bubbled underneath.

As Señora got the meeting focused again, Fiona raised her hand to be excused for soccer. Señora sighed and reluctantly let her leave.

"Before you go, what task team do you want to be on?" Señora asked as Fiona gathered her things.

Fiona said, "Food," without missing a beat.

Señora asked who else wanted to be a food volunteer. Almost every boy in the room raised his hand. Madison thought at first that was because they all wanted to be around Fiona. But it wasn't. These boys were just plain hungry.

After Fiona left, Señora began signing up names for the dance and music task team list. Aimee's hand shot into the air right away to be the dance task team leader. After all, she was the best dancer in seventh grade. It made the most sense. Not even Rose, Ivy's dancing drone, challenged Aimee when it came to this.

Aimee leaned over to ask Drew if he'd help pull together all the music, too. Drew's father was mega-rich. The Maxwells had a recording studio right there on their own property. He could make the best Halloween mix ever.

"Who would like to help lead our decorating crew?" Señora Diaz asked next. Ivy's hand went up. So did Madison's.

"Well." Señora seemed pleased by their double enthusiasm. "What do you each have to say?"

Ivy started talking as if she'd already been put in charge. "I think, as class president, I know what the decorating for our dance should be. I would like to organize decorations. And I really think I can handle the scary hallway setup, too . . ."

"Fair enough," Señora Diaz said. "Señorita Finn? Would you like to add anything?"

"Well . . . just . . ." Madison cleared her throat. "I just wanna say that—" The words got stuck on the way out.

"Madison," Ivy interrupted in her hideous, sticky-sweet voice. Madison's stomach curdled. "I really think we both know who'd be better at taking care of the decorating, don't we?"

Madison didn't know what to say to that.

But Aimee did.

"Excuse me," Aimee interrupted. Her face was blotchy and Madison feared she might haul out and punch Ivy right there. She looked *that* mad. Aimee took things very personally when it came to Poison Ivy.

"We do know who'd be better, Ivy. But I think Madison would like to give *you* a chance, too."

Gotcha!

Madison covered her mouth, surprised—and grateful.

Drew snorted again.

Ivy acted stunned.

"Now, girls," Señora chimed in. "I don't think we need that kind of talk." She looked squarely at both girls, squinting and thinking for a moment. Madison sat still. Ivy flipped her hair.

Señora spoke up. "There's more than enough work to go around for two or more people. I think Madison and Ivy should *both* lead this task team."

"What?" Ivy and Madison said at the same time. "You mean—"

"*Sí!*" Señora Diaz said in Spanish emphatically. "You will lead the decorating task team *together*. That is my final decision."

In one fleeting moment, Señora Diaz had sealed Ivy and Madison's Halloween dance fates. Now Madison and Poison Ivy weren't only partnered in science class—they were matched up *after* school, too.

The decorators worked on the to-do list for the

scary hallway first. It started out okay—without any fights or disagreements. Madison hoped it would stay that way. She scribbled some notes. Everyone had great ideas, and the meeting lasted over an hour. When Madison got home, the notes on her laptop became an official file on her laptop.

 Halloween Dance: To Do

- Get vibrating rubber hands with fake blood (Ivy)
- Plastic ax from props in basement
- Brain gelatin mold (home ec?)
- Eyeballs suspended from the ceiling (if possible)
- Sheets (everyone bring one set plus curtains)
- Sound effects music (esp. screaming—Mrs. Montefiore in the music dept.)
- Monster makeup (green, white clown makeup, black nail polish from Rose S.)
- Dry ice machine (Principal Bernard to help get)
- Bats, rats, and spiders (Madison)

Madison decided she'd be the best person to make spiders, roaches, and moths out of black and brown construction paper. Her love of animals and all things creepy-crawly made her perfect for the job.

Ivy decided that she wanted to put up all the balloons. Probably because the boys were already talking about playing with the helium machine. Madison wondered if that was Ivy's key motivation: blow up balloons, meet boys. Then again, everyone loved the idea of inhaling helium and talking like a squeaky Munchkin. Ivy always did things that were popular.

Suddenly Madison's e-mail box blinked. It even had a red exclamation mark next to it.

```
Importance: high!
From: Bigwheels
To: MadFinn
Subject: Happy Columbus Day?
Date: Tues 17 Oct 5:20 PM
I know I'm like 2 wks late, but did
I say happy Columbus Day? Or is
that holiday just a bad joke? My
old camp friend said Columbus didn't
really discover America. Is that
true? I figured you'd know.


Mom & Dad are officially back
together. Did I tell you that
already? Dad bought her flowers
yesterday, so I am feeling happy.
They were roses. Mom keeps humming,
though, and it's getting on my
nerves.
```

How is that guy you have a crush
on? What is his name again? Write
back or else, okay?

Yours till the peanut butters,

Bigwheels

P.S. Do you have a Halloween dance
at your school? I have to make
cupcakes for mine. I bet you're
making posters for the dance on
your computer, you're so good at
that artistic stuff.

P.P.S. What are you dressing up as
for Halloween?

**Madison clicked REPLY immediately. Sometimes
the way she and Bigwheels thought and talked
about the same things was** *scary*. **Her keypal hadn't
guessed that Madison would be on the decoration
committee, but anything else she talked about was
so true.**

From: MadFinn
To: Bigwheels
Subject: Re: Happy Columbus Day?
Date: Tues 17 Oct 6:10 PM
Hi!!!!! Thanks for writing back &
for your advice.

To answer all your comments and questions in order (sort of):

1. Happy Columbus Day to you, too.
2. There are some people who think Columbus wasn't the only guy. That's true. My mom almost produced a documentary on that subject. (Did I tell you that she makes movies? Mostly nature stuff, but sometimes profiles on famous people, too, like Christopher Columbus.)
3. I am so happy about your parents. WOW!
4. My crush is doing okay (see my question below).
5. We DO have a Halloween dance. I can't believe you asked me that question! We just met about it today. I was put on the decorating committee, BUT there's just one problem (see my question).

Now my questions for you.

1. How can I get my enemy (you know) away from the guy I like? She's after him, I know it!
2. How can I be on a dance committee when my enemy is in

charge? She's everywhere I go.
Help!!!

Okay, that's all for now. Bye!
WRITE BACK.

Yours till the scare crows,

MadFinn

P.S. Do you make up scary stories
or just poems? Just curious.
Bigfishbowl is having a special
Halloween writing contest. Are you
entering?

She clicked SEND and watched the e-mail disappear. Madison was thinking about how great it would be if Bigwheels wrote something for the contest, too.

But then Madison thought some more.

What would it be like to compete against a keypal at that contest? Competition got in the way of everything. Competing with Ivy for the decorations committee and for Hart was enough for one day.

Let the Halloween games begin.

Chapter 3

As soon as Madison arrived home from school the next day, she yanked her nubby brown sweater from the closet and down over her head. Her hair got static-electrified when she did that. She had an entire halo of split ends.

It was extra chilly in the house. Fall was beginning to make moves toward winter.

Madison wanted to power up her laptop and open her new file called "Caught in the Web." She had spent a half hour trying to write a story for the Halloween Web contest on her favorite site during free time in Mrs. Wing's class.

Unfortunately, she had zero ideas.

She also had zero time. Her dad and his new girlfriend, Stephanie, Madison, and Aimee were going on a late afternoon trip to Peterson's Farm. The four of them were going to get pumpkins and cider, a Finn tradition begun by Dad and his family years ago.

Madison had invited Fiona to come along, too, but Fiona had an important soccer practice (again).

Peterson's Farm was a half hour outside of Far Hills in a town called West Lake. There wasn't actually much of a lake there anymore, but when Dad was little, his parents brought him there every summer to swim and every winter to ice skate. Within a mile of the place, Dad usually got nostalgic.

"Do I look fat in this sweater, Mom?" Madison asked, walking back into the kitchen. She'd chosen brown corduroys to color-coordinate her bottom with the top.

"You look nice and warm," Mom said, ignoring the fat part of the question. "Now, don't forget to get me some of that corn relish at the farm, okay? And wear your Timberlands, not those sneakers. It's muddy out."

"It should be *you* going with us, Mom," Madison said, picking at cookies that had been left on the kitchen counter. "It's just not the same anymore . . ."

"Maddie," Mom said. She stopped what she was doing, leaned over, and gently rubbed a finger behind Madison's ear. "Look, Maddie, I know it's hard. I know this is the first real fall since your father and I split up—"

Madison rolled her eyes, so Mom grabbed her gently by the shoulders.

"Madison, later on this week you and I will do something that's fun just for us. Like making pies— or raking all the leaves in the backyard."

"Raking? That's your idea of fun?" Madison moaned. "Are you kidding?"

"Of course I'm only kidding!" Mom looked right into Madison's eyes again. It felt like she was staring right through her skin, bones, and everything.

Madison didn't feel like talking all of a sudden. She just hugged Mom.

"Honey bear," Mom continued to speak. "You'll love going up to West Lake. I know it. And you like Dad's girlfriend . . . what's her name?"

"Stephanie," Madison said. Mom sometimes forgot little details like names.

"Yes, *Stephanie*," Mom repeated slowly. "Well, you said you like her. What's the problem?"

"She's just not you," Madison said.

Mom squeezed her daughter around the middle. "Do me a favor and try to have a good time, Maddie. Try."

Tap tap.

Aimee was outside the kitchen door, face pressed so her lips went splat like a big guppy mouth kissing the glass. She'd changed her outfit since school, too.

Tap tap tap tap.

"I'm coming!" Madison said, opening the sliding doors.

31

"Hiya!" Aimee blurted, dancing inside. "Hey, Mrs. Finn!"

When she said "Finn," Phin, the dog, came running to say hello.

"Well, Aimee," Mom said. "Don't you look as pretty as always!"

Aimee grinned and struck one of her dancer poses. "Thank you."

"And that's a nice sweater," Madison said, rolling her eyes and half laughing. "Is it new?"

Aimee was wearing a black ski sweater with a big purple stripe.

"Oh my God, *this*? Not even. And it makes me look so *huge*," Aimee quipped. "You're not supposed to wear stripes across. Totally unflattering. But I thought it would be warm, so I wore it. It's wicked cold out today."

"You've got a lot of energy this afternoon," Mom declared.

"My brother Roger made me herbal tea when I got home from school," Aimee said. "You know how he always makes these drinks with ginger and ginseng. It's good for you."

Madison had never eaten or drunk anything with ginseng in it. It sounded too mysterious. She glanced at her own outfit and compared it to what Aimee had on. Aimee always seemed to dress the part of cool while Madison usually felt uncool in comparison.

Honk honk.

Aimee peeked out the window. "It's your dad, Maddie! Bye, Mrs. Finn!"

"That was good timing, huh?" Madison said, looking at Mom. It seemed hard to believe Dad was in the driveway on time. Mom said that in fifteen years of marriage, Jeff Finn had *never* been on time.

Dad stuck his head out the window to wave to Mom, who was standing on the porch. Mom waved limply and walked back inside.

Approaching the car, Madison saw Stephanie seated in the front seat. Stephanie had been riding up front since she'd begun dating Dad. Madison had a sinking feeling she would *never* ride shotgun in Dad's car again.

Madison and Aimee jumped in the back.

"How was school today, girls?" Dad asked, pumping the gas pedal. He started driving and asking so many questions that Madison was sure he must have had six cups of coffee. Dad was like a little kid when he got excited.

"So we have the entire afternoon planned out," Dad explained. "First the pumpkin patch—then cider—hmmm—what time is it, Stephanie?"

Stephanie turned to the girls in the backseat and winked as she said to Dad, "Slow down, will ya, Speed Racer? It's almost four o'clock."

The two friends chuckled. The farm closed up shop after six. They had plenty of time to get there and find the right pumpkins.

"Your dad got a new digital camera that we're going to try out," Stephanie said. "Did he tell you, Maddie?"

Dad spied Madison in the rearview mirror and smiled. "You up for a photo session, girls?"

"Yeah, I guess. I'm sure Aimee is," Madison teased.

"Hey!" Aimee laughed. "Well, I don't mind having my picture taken, if that's what you're asking, Mr. Finn." She gave Madison's shoulder a gentle nudge.

"That's good!" he said.

"How come you guys aren't at work or something?" Aimee asked.

Stephanie laughed. "Aren't days off a wonderful thing? We had a business meeting this morning. Saved the afternoon for you two."

"We'll beat the Saturday rush at the farm," Dad said. "You girls finished your homework like we agreed, right?"

Madison and Aimee nodded from the backseat.

Outside the car, tree branches shook their dead yellow, red, and orange leaves off in the wind. Madison pressed her nose up to the window on the passenger side and watched as her warm breath fogged up the cool glass. She traced a smiley face with her index finger. Aimee leaned over and used her fingers to draw squiggles in the same spot.

Soon they were driving through the farm gates.

After they parked, Dad led them to the horse cart transporting guests into the pumpkin patches.

Madison, Aimee, and Stephanie posed for a photo op in front of "Megasquash," a display of enormous zucchinis. Aimee stuck a piece of hay in her mouth and twirled around, working overtime to be the center of attention. Madison laughed hysterically while Dad clicked away.

The greatest thing about Dad's digital camera was that he could eliminate or retake bad pictures right away. Madison already guessed which picture she'd be downloading as a screen saver for her laptop. She and Aimee had hammed it up with a scarecrow in overalls.

The air on the farm smelled more and more like everything fall was supposed to smell like: horses, smoke from a chimney, apples, more hay. Madison took a deep breath of cool air. It was getting duskier outside.

"Look at this one, Maddie! It has boobs!" Aimee screeched when they jumped off the cart into the pumpkin patch. She held up a giant orange pumpkin with two funny-looking bumps on the side.

Madison laughed and ran over to join Aimee. They sorted through plump ones, round ones, flat ones, and even green ones. Stephanie found a teeny patch that had been picked over already by some crows. Dad found a pumpkin so big that it barely fit in the wagon they were using.

At five o'clock, Madison and Aimee ordered cups of cider at one of the farm stands and sat out on a picnic bench, even though it was a little too chilly to sit in one place for very long.

"How did you meet Mr. Finn?" Aimee asked, blowing on the cider before taking her first sip. She was so good at asking the right questions. Madison envied Aimee's ability to say whatever was on her mind.

Stephanie said that she was a computer sales rep. and met Madison's dad at a technology conference a few months back. In her head, Madison tried to do the math just to make sure that Dad had started dating Stephanie *after* the big D.

They had.

"Steph—" Dad started to groan. "Do you girls really wanna hear this?"

"Of course we do, Mr. Finn!" Aimee blurted. "Every detail. Like, what were you wearing when you met?"

"I think I had on a gray sweater." Stephanie chuckled. "And plaid pants."

"Plaid? Ohhh!" Aimee bristled like plaid was bad. She continued with her questions. "Have you ever been married before?"

Madison couldn't believe Aimee would ask something so personal.

Stephanie smiled. "Well, not exactly."

"What does 'not exactly' mean?" Madison asked.

"Well, here's the thing. I was engaged," Stephanie said. "Once. I was engaged, but I didn't go through with it. Couldn't go through with it."

"And am I glad for that," Dad said, wrapping his arm around Stephanie's back and leaning in to kiss her head.

Dad looked up just in time to see the expression on Madison's face. It was a "why did you just do that?" look. It had taken Madison her whole life to get used to Dad kissing Mom. Now she had to get used to Dad kissing someone else?

Eeeeeuuuw.

Madison remembered to grab a jar of Mom's favorite relish as they left the farm. She triple-checked the label to make sure it was the correct kind: extra spicy, Peterson's specialty.

Dad paid for all the pumpkins, including the one with boobs, and the relish, and then the foursome headed back to his Far Hills loft. He was preparing a "Finn Feast," or so he said. Stephanie promised she'd toast pumpkin seeds.

While Madison's dad and Stephanie cooked dinner, Madison logged on to Dad's newfangled computer with its slick chrome edges. Aimee just watched at first. Then she sat down and grabbed the mouse.

"Let's go to that fish site you were talking about yesterday," Aimee said. "With Fiona. You know the one."

"You mean bigfishbowl.com?" Madison asked.

Aimee nodded. "I wanna get a screen name. Can we do it now? Tonight?"

Madison smiled. After all this time, she was so happy to hear that Aimee wanted to log on for real. It meant the three friends could gab on the computer in three-way conversations. Finally. They signed on under Madison's screen name to start. Madison punched in her secret password.

The home page was a giant advertisement for the Caught in the Web Halloween story contest, with flashing spiders and cobwebs and witches floating past on on-screen broomsticks. If you moved the cursor over one of the fish inside the bowl, you saw its skeleton.

All at once, a shaded green box popped up. The cursor blinked quickly.

ENTER SCREEN NAME

"I don't know what my name should be, Maddie. Whaddya think? Twinkle toes?" Aimee joked. "Bertha big butt? Ha! You're good at nicknames. You gave Egg his nickname, didn't you?"

Madison laughed out loud. "Yeah, right." She had.

They punched in a perfect screen name for Aimee's personality.

BALLETGIRL

The screen flashed like a strobe light.

NAME TAKEN. SELECT ANOTHER. MAY WE RECOMMEND BALLETGIRL12?

"That's lame. What's the twelve for?" Aimee

asked, disappointed. "Are there really eleven other ballerinas on this Web site? I don't get this."

"Wait!" Madison exclaimed, punching in a different name without any numbers. She typed "BALLETGRL"—without the *I* for a change.

That worked.

At long last, Aimee was an official online member of the bigfishbowl community. She announced her name and her password out loud as she punched it in, like she was ordering something at the deli.

"BALLETGRL! POINTE!"

Aimee had a hard time keeping secrets. Even her own.

After dinner, the duo signed online again to test Aimee's new membership privileges in chat rooms and beyond. When Madison noticed that Wetwinz was online, she helped Aimee send her first Insta-Message ever.

They asked Fiona about soccer practice that day, and Fiona wrote back in an instant:

I can't believe this is YOU! That is so wow. C u!

"What's that?" Aimee asked, pointing to the letters *C* and *U* at the end of the message. She didn't understand Web lingo yet.

"C U. It's 'See you.' Get it? It's like computer shorthand. You'll pick it up after a while."

Then Madison took her turn logging in. Dad poked his head into the room to say it was time to pack up for home. Madison ran to the bathroom, leaving Aimme to surf the site by herself.

Aimee was zoned out on bigfishbowl.com, clicking from screen to screen, searching for a chat room. She couldn't believe the made-up names she encountered: ChuckD4Ever, PrtyGrrl88, and Brbiedoll.

All of a sudden, there was an Insta-Message up on the screen.

"Hey!" Aimee cried out to Madison. "What's this?"

"Huh?" Madison asked, walking back in.

"Who is Bigwheels?" Aimee said, eyes locked on the screen.

Chapter 4

 Aimee

My BFF finally got online! But here's
the problem—Bigwheels was online at the
exact same time!

Aimee was sitting there staring at the
Bigwheels Insta-Message on my dad's computer
screen. I just flipped. I hit DELETE and
told Aim it must be a wrong screen name,
like a wrong number on the phone. Then I
punched the RESET key and the computer went
black. Why didn't I just tell her?

Rude Awakening: The truth IS out there.
I'm just not ready to share it yet.

Thursday afternoon, Madison was *still* feeling
weirder than weird about avoiding Bigwheels

online. It was like the flu. She couldn't shake it. What was the big deal about telling Aimee that Bigwheels existed, anyway?

She looked away from the computer screen to see if the librarian or anyone else was loitering in the school media center. She was up here in the middle of a Thursday test block. Her teacher, Mr. Sweeney, had given her one of those "get out of math free" cards. Madison always tried to play her cards right, which usually meant finding a computer somewhere. She loved the chance to escape into her files, even if it was only for the briefest moment.

Once again she scanned the room to make sure no one was staring her way or spying.

Madison punched the side of her computer power tower with her fist to get it thumping and chugging, but that didn't help much. The media center machine was a real dinosaur. Hitting it only made the monitor buzz like some kind of angry, prehistoric insect.

From across the library where she was typing, Madison saw the flash of someone entering the library and did a double take. Most seventh-grade kids were at lunch, class, or study hall right now. The eighth- and ninth-grade classes were away on a day trip into the city.

Who was that?

It was hard not to be a little bit paranoid.

As soon as she saw funny hair sticking out all over the place, Madison felt better. She knew that head. It was Drew, standing by the biography section.

Madison waved and turned back to her files. But she heard something else. Breathing.

"Boo!"

Madison leaped out of her chair.

"You should watch what you write when people are around, Maddie." It was Egg. And he was breathing, right behind her—with lousy milk breath on top of everything else.

"Egg, you stink," Madison gasped. She meant it both ways.

"Yeah, but I gotcha!" Egg cackled like he'd just played the best trick ever. "When are you gonna get a clue? I GOTCHA!"

He was so good at scaring the wits out of her and everyone else whenever he got the chance.

From across the room, Drew smiled wide. Was he laughing? Madison frowned. No more Little Miss Nice Guy with any of these boys, Madison thought. Drew was probably just Egg's lookout.

She had been tricked.

"Whatcha doing?" Egg asked. "What *are* you writing?"

"None of your beeswax, Egg. You are so nosy!"

Madison hid the computer monitor screen with both palms pressed flat and quick-saved her document. She pulled her disk out of the computer and casually shoved it into her orange bag.

"Maddie, why are you always up here alone?" Egg asked. "You living up here or what?"

Drew walked over. "Er . . . Egg, the bell's about to ring."

"I'm going to get you guys back for this." Madison pursed her lips. "*Both* of you."

"Yeah right." Egg cackled again. "For your information, I'm not a little scaredy-cat. . . ."

"Egg, the bell's going to ring any minute." Drew tugged on Egg's sleeve.

"Yeah, yeah." Egg moaned.

Madison got up to walk away.

"Hey, wait up!" Egg called after her. "You didn't answer my question."

"You didn't *ask* a question," Madison grumbled. She kept right on walking, out of the library and into the main stairwell. Whatever it was that Egg had to say, Madison wasn't in the mood. She already felt bad enough with the whole lying-to-Aimee thing. She didn't need Egg trouble!

Madison made her way to science class. The room was chaos today, with kids talking and standing everywhere except their assigned seats. There was no teacher in sight. Madison slipped uncomfortably into her assigned seat next to Poison Ivy.

On the other side of Ivy, Hart sat perched on his lab stool, nose in his notebook. Madison tried to catch his eye, just to say hello, but she couldn't see him and he couldn't see her. Every time she leaned forward, Ivy leaned forward. Whenever she pushed backward, Ivy pushed back, too.

Hart was out of reach and out of sight.

The worst part about Hart being so close and yet so far was all the secondhand listening. Ivy and Hart were having one of those drippy, flirty conversations.

"Whassup?"

"Not much. Whassup with you?"

"Nothing."

"So . . . what's going on?"

"Nothing. What's going on with—"

Drip, drip, DRIP!

Madison screamed inside her own head. She couldn't understand why Hart was so nice to Ivy. Was he worked up over Ivy's red, flowing hair? Was he under some kind of weird spell? (It was Halloween, after all.)

Or worst of all—did he like her?

That would be a real nightmare.

Five minutes after class should have begun, their regular teacher Mr. Danehy, still hadn't arrived. A joker standing in the middle of the room said there was some kind of ten-minute rule they could follow if the teacher wasn't there soon. No teacher after ten minutes meant class was automatically canceled. Madison wished for that. It would be like getting a "get out of class free" card, only better. It meant escape from Poison Ivy.

Chet took the delay as another opportunity to stand up in front of the class and act like a clown. He liked to pretend he was the teacher, testing his bad imitation of Mr. Danehy's unidentifiable accent.

In the middle of all the fuss, the door to room 411 opened with a whoosh.

Chet froze. He thought he'd been caught red-handed in the act of impersonating a teacher.

But Mr. Danehy wasn't the one standing there. It was a substitute teacher from central casting. And he was taller than tall.

Everyone scurried into their seats and shut up.

The big guy who'd arrived on the scene was wearing an average-looking white shirt, loose green tie, and khaki pants. But he was anything but ordinary. He leaned against the doorway casually so his head almost hit the top of the frame. Madison figured he must be seven feet tall.

"Hello, seventh-grade science class," the big guy grunted as he entered, eyes scanning the room. Everyone in class nodded back like a bunch of robots. They weren't sure who this was, but they knew he wasn't someone to mess with. "I'm Mr. Stein," he said gruffly, writing it up on the board. *"S-t-e-i-n."*

He stepped back with a clop, kicking a wadded-up piece of paper on the floor. His hair was a jet-black helmet. The only thing missing was bolts in his neck.

"Did you say you were Mr. Stein?" Chet blurted. "As in Frank-en-stein?" He chuckled at his own joke.

Mr. Stein chuckled right back. "Not Frank. *Bob.*"

"Ha!" Chet burst out laughing. "That's funny!"

"Yeah, well," Mr. Stein continued. "I'm the funny science sub. What can I say? Now, let's get to work."

The rest of the class laughed out loud as Mr. Stein told a couple more jokes about werewolves. Then he asked everyone to pull out their textbooks. He wrote the formal assignment from Mr. Danehy on the board.

Read pages 101 to 151.

"I know that's a lot for thirty minutes, so do as much reading as is humanly possible," Mr. Stein urged, shuffling a few papers in front of him. "But no talking, okay?" He sat down at Mr. Danehy's desk with a thunk.

Chet leaned over to Hart and whispered, "Am I crazy, or is this guy a walking science experiment?"

Madison sighed audibly. "Shhh!" She opened her textbook to do the reading. There had been enough monstrous moments for one day.

A few minutes later, however, kids got restless. First they started to mumble. Despite Mr. Stein's instructions, whispering came over the room like a breeze. Madison was trying as hard as she could *not* to listen to any of it, but she couldn't help overhearing Ivy's whispers to Hart because they were just a foot away.

"Hart, are you asking anyone to the Halloween dance?" Ivy was using her soft, sweet voice.

"Nah," Hart answered. "I'm just gonna go with some friends."

Ivy leaned in closer. "You can ask someone if you want. To the dance, I mean."

"Yeah," Hart said. "But I don't wanna."

"Do you wanna help on a dance committee?" Ivy asked. "You were at the meeting, weren't you? What task team are you on?"

"Not sure yet," he said.

"Why don't you help with decorations, Hart? You could help hang up stuff. I bet you'd be really good. That's the committee I'm on."

Madison thought she saw Ivy press her leg against Hart's leg, but she wasn't so sure. Were there rules about that? Hart's knee looked a little jumpy.

He cleared his throat. "Did you say decorations? Well . . . that sounds kinda . . . well . . . not for me. Thanks anyway."

"You could do the scary hallway, Hart. That's an important job."

"I guess—look—"

"Please," Ivy begged. "Pretty, pretty, *pretty* please."

Madison knew Poison Ivy was using her whole bag of tricks to get Hart on her side. She even smelled like flowered perfume. Ivy knew 101 ways to

48

get boys to do things. She'd say *anything* to get what she wanted.

"Okay, okay," Hart said. "I guess I could be on a decoration committee. Just cool out, all right? I gotta do this science now."

Madison couldn't hear the rest of what was being said—only that Ivy laughed. And Hart laughed right back.

Was he laughing at her or with her?

And there was his knee, still bouncing up and down like a jackhammer. Was he nervous? Having a seizure? Madison dreaded the thought that Hart was actually in the middle of liking Poison Ivy Daly right there in front of Mr. Stein and everyone else in science class. Madison couldn't take her eyes off that leg.

"Hey! What are *you* looking at?" Ivy snarled. She'd caught Madison staring. She *always* caught Madison staring. Ivy flipped her red hair and leaned in. "It's rude to stare, you know. You're being *rude*, Madison."

But Hart's legs were still moving—*bounce, bounce, bounce.*

Madison secretly wished he would just fall off his stool.

Chapter 5

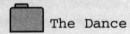 The Dance

Rude Awakening: This Halloween is turning into Shalloween.

They should put warning labels on people. Since Ivy joined the decorating team, the Halloween dance is doomed. She sits in our meetings with her pink cell phone sticking out of her bag and her nose stuck up in the air and I could just scream! Anytime anyone said anything, she was like, "I don't think that's a good idea."

Not only that, but I saw her outside the cafeteria (she didn't see me) talking to this cute boy, Nick, about helping with the dance. She wanted to know if he had a date. A DATE?

There's no dating! This dance is for
EVERYONE, not just couples. Right???
   I wonder why Hart hasn't called me
Finnster in a long time. Has he forgotten?
I know I hate it when he calls me that,
but I kinda miss it.

Madison hit SAVE and looked up to see the clock on top of Mrs. Wing's filing cabinets.

It was two forty-eight.

She had twelve minutes to go before the last bell of the day rang. Today was one of the most anticipated soccer games of the school season—the one scheduled against Far Hills' biggest rival school, Dunn Manor. Madison was meeting Aimee down at the lockers right after the final bell. Most of the seventh grade would be in attendance, screaming and rooting for their favorite infielders. They wanted to cheer the loudest. Aimee was even skipping her dance troupe practice for today's game.

It had been a hugely successful soccer season for Fiona and the rest of the Far Hills Rangers. The entire team was touted as an early contender for the district championships, and today's match was supposed to be closer than close. The only minor problem was the rain. The Far Hills soccer field would be a little muddy, since it had been drizzling all day. Madison didn't mind, but Aimee was obsessing about her hair frizzing.

"Bummer! I can't believe it's raining." Aimee

groaned, opening her locker. Inside she had a mirror glued to the door. She combed her hair and applied a dab of all-natural lip gloss. She extended the container to Madison. "Try some."

Madison shook her head. "Since when do you wear makeup?"

"Gloss is not *really* considered makeup," Aimee said. "Besides, this company doesn't test on animals. So it's cool. And it tastes like candy."

Madison stuck her finger into the little pot of gloss. It was better than the strawberry kiwi smooch stuff she'd used in the past. She smacked her lips. They did shimmer. And they tasted like purple lollipops.

Aimee brushed her blond hair some more. Madison just laughed. "What's the point, Aimee We're just going to get wet anyhow."

Madison adjusted her own ponytail and Aimee closed her locker. Dozens upon dozens of students, parents, and teachers were moving out the front doors down to the soccer field.

Even with the light rain, seventh, eighth *and* ninth graders showed up. Most kids ignored the drizzle, but parents sat holding umbrellas. The game hadn't started yet. Players from both teams were milling about on the field.

Madison flailed her arms to catch Fiona's attention, but Fiona didn't see. She was in the middle of putting on her shin guards. Madison pulled her hand down quickly so no one would spot her waving to someone who wasn't waving back.

"Go, Far Hills! Go, Fiona!" Aimee screeched. She would have danced around, too, but it was very damp and cramped where they were sitting. Instead she just twirled her hips and screamed.

Aimee's screeches and moves were as embarrassing to Madison as her own waving incident. Every time Aimee said something or did something, Madison was sure kids turned around to stare. She wanted to dive under the bleachers—and run back to her locker.

"Look! There's Egg and Chet!" Aimee yelled their names. *"EGG! CHET!"*

They didn't hear. They were down closer to the field, talking to a couple of seventh-grade girls. Chet had his hands in his pockets, and one girl was tugging on his sleeve. Madison couldn't hear them but she knew exactly what they were talking about. It was like the Ivy-and-Hart conversation in science class.

Madison wished that she could learn to flirt like Ivy and the girls who were talking to Egg and Chet.

The Rangers were huddled in a semicircle by the sideline bench. The opposing team, the Mallards, did the same, arms locked, shirts dripping wet. The only difference between the two huddles was that the Rangers were outfitted in blue and white while the Mallards were sporting red-and-gold uniforms. Girls from both teams had mud on their legs even though they hadn't started the game yet.

Whoooooooooooooo!

Someone blew a whistle and a roar exploded from below. Both sides were clapping as they took the field. Everyone in the stands clapped, too. Fiona and the rest of the Rangers looked superconfident. There weren't very many cheers for Dunn Manor, just a small group of boys and girls closer to the bottom of the bleachers. Madison saw someone's dad holding a yellow sign that said WE'RE NOT DUNN UNTIL WE BEAT FAR HILLS!

Madison felt a surge of irresistible energy being there. Soon she was cheering as loudly as Aimee.

"Go, Rangers," everyone shrieked together. "Go! Go! Go!"

By now Egg, Drew, and Chet had found Madison and Aimee in the stands. They pushed their way up to their rows.

"Yo!" Egg screamed. "This is so awesome, right? Better than those middle-school games."

Egg and Drew whistled the kind of whistle where they stuck their two fingers into their mouths. It was way louder than the plain old pucker whistle that Madison was trying.

Chet screamed, and everyone looked down onto the soccer field in time to see a Mallard take off with the ball. But there was no shot at goal.

Not yet. But Fiona was on the move.

"There she goes!" Chet screamed. It was funny, Madison thought, to see him looking so happy, almost proud, at what his sister was doing. In spite of the fact that he was the most annoying part of her life, Chet and Fiona were so totally bonded. Madison couldn't imagine what it would be like to have a twin.

Fiona raced up and down the soccer field in the spitting rain. She got her chance to kick on goal—but missed. The crowd sighed together.

That's when Madison saw Hart. He was wearing a Far Hills sweatshirt. He never looked up, so he had no idea Madison was there, but she kept her eyes glued on him. She scanned the area around him, but no Ivy.

"Madison, isn't this the best?" Aimee squealed. "I came to soccer games before with my brothers, and it was never like this."

Everyone around them took a deep breath at the exact same time.

"Ahhhh!"

The crowd howled as the Rangers jumped around on the field. There was a penalty and an off-side kick. The crowd waited. The clock ticked. Fiona kicked.

"Goal!"

The ball flew right into the goal net. She was a star! The Mallards' goalie collapsed into the mud. She looked madder than mad.

"Woooooooo!" Aimee jumped up and started to

do a wave, only no one else followed. This time Madison didn't care.

By the time the soccer game ended, the Rangers were the hands-down winners with a score of 2–0. Fiona and another wing named Daisy Espinoza had scored the game-winning goals. Teammates slapped each other's backs and said, "Good game, good game, good game." Madison could hear them from where she was sitting. This victory meant the team would go on to the district championships, the first time in twelve years for Far Hills.

Madison and Aimee hurried down the bleachers to find Fiona.

"You won the game!" Madison said the moment she spied her soccer star friend.

"Thanks for coming," Fiona said. Her blue-and-white shirt was soaked through. "Hey, you guys, have you seen my mother? She was supposed to come, too."

"Great job!" Mrs. Waters said, appearing out of nowhere. She hugged Fiona tight. Chet was right behind, ready to give his sister a high five.

Everyone was shivering and laughing at the same time. The coach came up to congratulate Mrs. Waters on her daughter's success.

"Nice kicking," Chet said.

Fiona couldn't stop grinning. She looked so happy doing what she did best. It was the same look Aimee had after dance recitals.

"So are you girls coming to our Halloween sleep-over tomorrow?" Mrs. Waters asked.

Chet laughed. "Girl party! Maybe I should invite some guys over, Ma."

"Chet Waters!" Mrs. Waters said. "Why don't you just go help Fiona get her stuff over to the car?"

"He's not going to be there." Fiona leaned in to whisper to Aimee and Madison. "My brother is such a geek."

"We're definitely coming." Aimee grinned. "I would never miss a sleepover. It's really nice of you to have us over, Mrs. Waters. Thank you."

"I can't wait," Madison said. "Hope it's not a dark and stormy night or anything like that."

"Like today!" Mrs. Waters laughed.

Madison looked upward and drops pelted down onto her face. She stuck out her tongue and swallowed a little bit of rain, cool and warm at the same time.

"Why don't I give you girls a ride home?" Mrs. Waters said, trying in vain to hold her umbrella out over Madison and Aimee. The rain was coming down harder now. Everyone ran to the Waterses' minivan.

Madison saw Hart again as she was running, but he didn't see her. Actually, she saw Egg and Drew standing there, too, but she didn't wave like she'd done with Fiona earlier in the afternoon. One non-returned wave was enough for one day. It would be twice as mortifying if Hart was the one who didn't wave back.

"Race ya!" Aimee said to Fiona as they approached the minivan. She leaped over a puddle gracefully, as only a dancer could.

"Last one there is a rotten—" Fiona was already halfway to the car.

Madison stayed back and walked more slowly alongside Mrs. Waters. She was afraid that if she ran, she might fall and land right on her wet behind, right in the middle of the deepest puddle.

Madison didn't want to risk any more embarrassing episodes around Hart Jones—or anyone else.

After a Chinese takeout dinner with Mom, Madison logged on to bigfishbowl.com home page. The writing contest deadline was fast approaching, and she needed to get some work done on her story.

If only she had some ideas.

```
Enter the Caught in the Web Contest
TODAY!
First Prize: Your Story on the Web
plus a mystery game (valued at
$25)!
```

The site flashed brighter and faster than she'd remembered. Fortunately the contest deadline had been extended by a couple of days. That made her breathe easier. It gave her more time to make her story scary. She needed all the time she could get.

While online, her Insta-Message box blinked. It was Bigwheels!

They met in GOFISHY, their favorite chat room.

```
<Bigwheels>: Ur online!
<MadFinn>: Didja get my EMSG?
<Bigwheels>: Y
<MadFinn>: ggg
<Bigwheels>: Howz dance comitee
<Bigwheels>: committee (sorry)
<MadFinn>: ok. SHE'S still around
    but whatever
<Bigwheels>: who?
<MadFinn>: IVY MY ENEMY
<Bigwheels>: IC
<MadFinn>: :>(
<Bigwheels>: Howz Hart?
<MadFinn>: He's :-9
<Bigwheels>: I wish I had a BF
<MadFinn>: Wait a minute, he's NO
    WAY my BF
<MadFinn>: N e way, I have to
    forget him, I think my chances
    are like NONE
<Bigwheels>: Don't say that! I've
    never met you F2F but I bet ur
    cool and pretty
<MadFinn>: Whatever—he likes HER I
    know
<Bigwheels>: Other fish in the sea
    then
```

<MadFinn>: Like on bigFISHbowl? LOL
<Bigwheels>: ;-]
<MadFinn>: Are you entering that
   contest on the home page of this
   site
<Bigwheels>: Huh?
<MadFinn>: CAUGHT IN THE WEB
<Bigwheels>: No u asked me that
   already
<MadFinn>: Oh I am
<Bigwheels>: What's ur story gonna
   be? I can't write stories only
   poems I think should I write a
   poem?
<MadFinn>: I want to write something
   scary
<Bigwheels>: Why don't you write
   about that GIRL who's ur enemy @
   school she sounds scary
<MadFinn>: Good idea!!! Or I could
   write about my life . . . LOL
<Bigwheels>: Yeah IMO real life is
   the scariest thing
<MadFinn>: :-0
<Bigwheels>: Good nite
<MadFinn>: Sleep tight!
<Bigwheels>: *poof*

Chapter 6

"You want gravy on that?" the lunch lady, Gilda Z, asked, ladle in one hand and giant fork in the other.

Madison stared down at her tray. Was this mystery meat moving?

Gilda slopped on gravy. Most landed on the tray, not the plate. "Next!" she cried.

Madison moved along. She peered over her shoulder and saw Hart standing a few kids back. He was peeling a banana. For a split second, she pretended not to notice him. But it was too late.

"Hey, Finnster!" he called out. He'd spotted her. Even though she suddenly felt nervous to talk to him, she also felt relieved to hear his nickname for her.

"Hart? H-h-h-hey," Madison replied. Her lips quivered like Jell-O. Crushes can make a person speak gibberish sometimes. Madison was so crushed out.

"What's on the menu today?" Hart asked. He glanced down at Madison's plate. "Whoa, that meat loaf looks sick."

Madison's helping of meat loaf didn't look like real meat because it was absolutely the wrong color. The gravy didn't help. Gray-vee. It had a weird brown crust, too.

"Oh . . . not so bad with ketchup, maybe?" Madison smiled nervously. She wanted to say the right things in front of Hart. But all she could do was defend her lunch.

Hart made a loud "yeeeeech" noise. "You have more guts than me, Finnster. I'm having a bologna sandwich today." He cut ahead and moved down the line.

For dessert, Madison grabbed a cupcake with orange frosting. It was decorated like a jack-o-lantern on the top with chocolate chips for eyes. She asked Hart if he wanted one, too. He didn't.

"Um . . . do you want to sit at our table in the back?" Madison asked. She tried to say it casually, but it came out kind of forced. "Sit. Table. The orange one." She gestured like an orangutan who had just learned language.

Hart shrugged. "Yeah. Egg's there already. I can see him. Sure."

She followed him to the back of the cafeteria,

past the table where Poison Ivy and her drones were sitting.

"Hey, Hart," Ivy said.

He gave Ivy one of those guy nods and kept right on walking. She looked surprised. So was Madison.

Madison held her breath. She didn't want to do anything stupid like burst into a merry chorus of "nah-nah-nah-nah-nahs." She didn't dare look back.

When they reached the orange table, Hart stuck out his hand and Egg slapped it. The table was three-quarters full: Egg, Drew, Aimee, Fiona, Chet, and a few floaters at the other end. Hart squeezed in at the opposite end from Madison. Sadly, there would be no accidental knee knocking over lunch.

"How could you get that meat loaf, Maddie?" Aimee asked as soon as Madison had put down her tray. "It looks dead."

Everyone else leaned in to look. Apparently no one had gotten the lunch selection except for Madison.

"Do you even know what's in that?" Aimee stuck out her tongue. "I thought you liked animals."

"I didn't really think about it," Madison said, sticking her fork in it. The fork stood straight up. She threw a napkin over the whole thing. "I'll just eat yogurt, then."

Hart and Chet were laughing. Madison hoped it wasn't at her. She opened the yogurt container.

"Did you see the new posters for the Halloween dance?" Fiona asked. "I am so excited. Señora is calling it Cobwebs and Creeps."

"What is that supposed to be? Our theme?" Madison asked aloud. "I didn't know we had a theme."

"That's because you're too busy getting gross loaf," Egg said. Drew snort-laughed and the rest of the boys started laughing, too.

"Who's going dressed as what for Halloween?" Aimee asked the table.

Egg grinned. "A rapper. Totally."

"You should go as Jimmie J, Egg," Hart said. "Ladies' man."

Jimmie J was a heartthrob from a popular boy band. Madison never understood why he made girls swoon. He had such hairy arms.

"Why stop at Jimmie J, Egg? You should go as the *whole* band," Aimee teased. "But then again, you can't sing at all, so . . . maybe not . . ."

"Not!" Egg chuckled. "Very funny, Aim."

"Is everyone going trick or treating this year?" Chet asked. "Fiona and I always went when we lived in California, but I thought maybe this year was the year when we stopped. . . ."

"Stopped? Why wouldn't we go?" Drew said quickly.

Egg grinned. "Yeah. Somewhere out there is a bucket of candy with my name on it."

"I want *lots* of candy," Fiona declared.

"Last year I had an entire trashbagful of candy and it lasted through February," Hart said. "February! It's my own personal record."

"Man, I ate all my candy in only two days," Egg said. "And then I was dog sick for like a week."

Madison nodded. "I remember."

"I hate it when candy gets stale," Aimee complained. "I had to throw most of my candy out."

"What are you talking about, Aimee? You don't even eat candy," Drew said.

Aimee shrugged and took a bite of carrot.

"Don't you guys think we're a little old to go trick-or-treating?" Madison said. "I mean, I don't wanna sound like I'm a—"

"PARTY POOPER!" Egg yelled.

Aimee slapped Egg's shoulder. "I'm with you, Maddie," she said.

"Hey! I like trick-or-treating," Fiona said. "We're not too old!"

"Are you saying we have to stop trick-or-treating just because we're in junior high?" Egg said. "I intend to do it for as long as I possibly can. And after that, even."

"We have to wear costumes for the Halloween dance. Why not use 'em again to get good candy?" Drew said.

"Hey, know what? If I can't be a rapper, I wanna

dress up like a mummy," Egg said. "For my costume, I mean. For the dance."

"A mummy is *in* a wrapper. That's practically the same thing, right?" Drew laughed at his own lame joke.

"What if we all went trick-or-treating together?" Chet said. "Maybe we could go as a TV family or something. Like the Simpsons."

"I love them!" Madison said enthusiastically.

"What did you dress up as last year, Maddie?" Drew asked.

Madison thought for a moment. "I dunno," she mumbled.

Dressing up for Halloween always stressed out Madison.

"I think I'm going to dress up as a boxer this year," Chet said. "Or a martian. Yeah. Something freaky."

Fiona groaned. "You would. "

"I'm going to go to the dance as a ballerina," Aimee said. She picked at a lettuce leaf on her plate. Aimee was becoming the kind of person who counted peas before she ate them.

"Ballerina? Like that's a big surprise." Egg made a face.

"You should go as a wizard," Drew said to Hart. "You have the cape and hat from *The Wiz*, right?"

"Yeah, I do," Hart said. "Maybe I should go as a wizard."

"You were great as the wizard," Fiona said. "And you could do tricks at the dance. You're really good at tricks, Hart."

Egg sneered. "Magic, shmagic. I'm gonna be a ninja. What about you, Fiona?"

"I wanna be a hula dancer."

"Hula girl, whoa!" Egg teased. "You got a grass skirt?"

Fiona smiled at him and tilted her head slightly to the side. She'd been crushing on him for weeks, so she didn't mind his teasing one bit.

"Why don't you lend her *your* grass skirt, Egg!" Chet said, laughing.

Egg made a face.

"Remember when Egg dressed up like a doctor for Halloween?" Aimee asked the table.

Madison rolled her eyes. "That was like a million Halloweens ago—"

"When we were *six*—" Aimee said.

"And Egg got into a yelling match with these nasty kids walking down the street and—"

"Yeah, yeah, and I got picked off by an egg on the Fourth Street overpass." Egg shook his head. "Get to the point, Maddie. I got hit with an egg, so that's when you started calling me Egg. Thanks a lot."

"At least it wasn't toilet paper." Hart laughed. "T.P. would be a worse nickname."

The table snickered.

Madison looked up at the lunchroom clock. The bell was about to sound. She saw Ivy getting up a few tables away, probably heading for the girls' bathroom. Ivy looked right over at Madison and the rest of the orange table with a mean, hard stare. Madison was glad that Hart wasn't watching.

What tricks did Poison Ivy have up her Boop-Dee-Doop sleeves now?

Fiona, Aimee, and Madison got up to return their trays.

"Hey, Maddie, have you entered that fishbowl contest yet?" Fiona asked.

"Huh? Not yet." Madison shook her head.

"I've been going online a lot more," Aimee told her girlfriends.

"You have?" Fiona replied. She swallowed her last bite of chocolate pudding.

"Since I got my screen name, anyway," Aimee said. "It's fun going into those chat rooms. You were right."

Fiona and Madison smiled at Aimee. Finally she was getting wired.

"But I'm still a newbie." Aimee sighed.

"Don't worry," Fiona said, rubbing her friend's shoulder. "Hey, did you both ask your moms about going to the mall Saturday before our sleepover?"

"Yes!" Madison chirped. "Mom said as long as my room is clean. Which means yes."

68

"My mother said yes, too. She even said she'd take us! She needs to go to the health food outlet and run some other errands."

"This is going to be so cool." Fiona grinned.

Going to the mall was an event. Not only did it mean trying on and perhaps even buying clothes, it also meant eating tacos at the food court, being parent-free, and spying on cute boys across the atrium or on the escalators. The three girls started making a list of what stores they would visit.

"So now that you're online, are you going to enter the Caught in the Web contest?" Madison asked.

"Nah," Aimee said. "I'm just not a good writer like you, Maddie."

"Me neither," Fiona said.

"Well, thanks, but the truth is, I'm a little stuck for ideas," Madison finally admitted. "Do you think you could help?"

"Write about ghosts," Fiona said. "Ghosts are the traditional—"

"Duh! Ghosts aren't scary enough anymore, Fiona," Aimee interrupted. "How about zombies? They're like ghosts, only they *eat* people. Now, that's scary."

"And yucky." Madison laughed. "Once upon a time there was a flesh-eating zombie named Aimee. . . ."

"Why don't you ask my brother for a good

69

idea?" Fiona suggested as they returned to the orange table. "I mean, Chet's a big, fat, lazy zombie!"

The girls laughed loudly. Chet turned around when he heard his name, but he hadn't caught the insult.

Brrrrring.

The lunchroom bell finally rang. All the boys bolted out of the cafeteria without saying good-bye to the girls. It was the usual routine. The girls headed for the door.

Madison walked out slowly, waiting for a flash of brilliance. She was so impatient. She needed a perfect story idea right now.

What was scarier: today's meat loaf or Poison Ivy?

Phinnie was waiting behind the front door when Madison came home that afternoon. He pounced on her with his scratchy claws. She had to take him for a long walk. Mom was busy writing.

Madison looped around the neighborhood and wandered over to Ridge Road. Without even thinking, she turned down Fiona's block. Phin liked this street because so many other dogs lived nearby. His little pug nose was snorting and sniffling at each tree. Madison couldn't imagine what it would be like to smell so many things at one time.

She looked around at houses on the street, mostly old Victorians with front porches and wide front yards. There was no one else around moving—no cars, no people, not even another dog.

As they passed Fiona's house, Madison glanced up. She thought about how last year Fiona and her family didn't live there. So much had changed.

Madison stopped short and yanked back on Phinnie's leash. Even though Fiona's family had repainted, restored, and added on to the side of the old house, it still reminded Madison of stories she'd once heard about the family who used to live there. People always said the old Martin place was haunted.

"*Rowrrroooo!*" Phinnie barked and tugged, and Madison nearly fell over. She pulled back on the leash, but he still took off down the street to say hello to a neighbor's poodle.

Madison glanced back at the house and then quickly ran after Phin.

Chapter 7

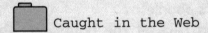 Caught in the Web

IT WAS A DARK AND STORMY NIGHT. THE
HOUSE WAS DEAD QUIET, EXCEPT FOR . . .
Aaaaaaaaaaaaaaaaaaaa!

Madison stared at the monitor, stuck. Her finger was pressing the *a* key over and over again. She remembered something her English teacher told her once about letting ideas go. Mr. Gibbons said to just "keep writing no matter what lands on the page." So she wrote whatever came into her head.

Here I am on bigfishbowl and I'm frozen.
Like a big fish stick.

Ick. It wasn't exactly the beginning of the scary story Madison was looking for. It was late Saturday morning, and Madison could hear Mom grinding coffee downstairs. The whole house smelled like hazelnuts.

Madison pulled her laptop over to her bed and lay down on her stomach to type. She was tired and wanted to surf the Net a little before going to the mall with Fiona and Aimee.

"Are you kidding me?" Mom shouted, walking into her room. "Look at this mess!"

Madison looked up from her laptop, surprised. "Mom!"

Her mother picked up a pile of clothes from near the doorway and dumped it in a wicker hamper a few feet away.

"Maddie, Aimee's mom will be here in a little while! Look at this *mess*! I said no mall until you clean your room—and I meant it!"

"But, Mom . . . I was just . . ." She closed the laptop lid and jumped up.

"I don't want to hear any excuses, Madison Finn. Pick up, get dressed, and get downstairs. And put that computer away! You have ten minutes."

Mom shut the bedroom door behind her.

Madison knew what to expect when she finally did head downstairs. In addition to a lecture about putting dirty clothes away and keeping her room clean, Madison would also get a minilecture on the perils of "computer overuse."

Quickly Madison cleaned up. She pushed some papers under the bed and shoved sneakers and shoes into the already overflowing closet. She couldn't miss going to the mall with friends—and without Mom. Besides, after shopping at the mall, she was going right over to Fiona's house for their spooky sleepover. She definitely couldn't miss that!

Madison stuffed some clean underwear, her Lisa Simpson nightshirt, jeans, and a sweatshirt for tomorrow into her bag.

Luckily Mrs. Gillespie was a few minutes late. It gave Madison more time to straighten up all her piles and make her bed neater. She even picked up Phin's toys off the floor.

When Mrs. Gillespie honked the car horn, Madison had passed the clean room test. She ran out to meet her friends.

Aimee and Fiona were bursting with energy when Madison climbed into the car, bouncing on the seats like they'd eaten way too much sugar.

The mall was crowded when they got there. Before Mrs. Gillespie scooted off to run her own errands, she told the girls to meet back at the North Fountain by four o'clock sharp.

As Aimee's mom walked away, the three friends bolted for Chez Moi—a casual boutique with faded

denim skirts and lace-up boots in the window. Aimee
wanted to try on what the mannequins were wearing. Madison wanted to head toward the back of the
store, where the hair scrunchies and jewelry were.
Fiona stopped and took a camouflage shirt off the
rack.

"For the warrior look," she said, laughing.
"Tarzan-ella."

Aimee grabbed it out of her hand and hung it
back up. She pulled out a cropped T-shirt with
sequins on the top that spelled FOXY, the same shirt
the mannequin had been wearing

"I like this one, don't you?" Aimee asked.

"My mother would never let me get that," Fiona
said.

"Well, your mom isn't here and neither is mine.
Try it on," Aimee said, pressing it into Fiona's hand
and taking one for herself and Madison. They scurried over to the changing rooms.

Fiona came out and modeled the T-shirt. Madison
could see muscles in Fiona's stomach, from soccer,
probably. Aimee had them, too, from dance. The
shirt fit Fiona perfectly everywhere else, too.

"You try it on now, Maddie," Fiona said, excited.
She grabbed Madison's arm and dragged her into
the dressing room.

Madison slipped the shirt over her head. It
looked okay around the middle even if Madison's
belly was softer looking, but the shirt hung down

lower than it had on Fiona. Madison wondered why.

"How's it look?" Aimee asked through the dressing room curtain. "Let's see!"

Madison stood sideways and backways and frontways in front of the mirror. The lights in the dressing room made her skin look almost green. She also thought the word FOXY was dumb. And there was absolutely nothing filling it out on top. Not like Fiona. Madison whipped the top off and stepped back out in her own loose shirt.

"It's not me. You should get it, though, Fiona. It looked so good on you."

"Ha! You're kidding, right? My dad wouldn't let me out of the house in this." Fiona put the top back on the rack. "Aimee's the one who should get it."

Aimee shrugged. "I don't have any allowance money left."

A salesperson meandered over toward them, so the friends turned to dash. They left Chez Moi and went to check out some other stores.

It was over an hour before Madison, Fiona, or Aimee saw even one person they recognized, which was strange, considering malls were the number-one place to see and be seen. Madison was especially surprised she didn't spy Poison Ivy anywhere.

Passing the food court, Madison saw Egg's sister, Mariah, sitting with friends. She could see the glimmer of Mariah's eyebrow ring. Her now black-dyed hair was wrapped in a polka-dotted bandanna.

She was all the way across the food court, so Madison couldn't yell. She wasn't sure if Mariah had seen her, anyway. Madison wanted to walk over and say hello, but Aimee wouldn't budge.

"You don't wanna do that, Maddie," Aimee said.

Madison looked puzzled. "Why not? Mariah is so nice. And she's your friend, too."

"She's all of our friends, Aimee," Fiona added.

"You guys!" Aimee moaned. "I know from my brothers that freshmen like her cannot be bothered to talk to lowly seventh graders like us except far away from school property, and the mall doesn't count. Besides, she's with boys from the high school, which makes it that much worse. It would just be too, too embarrassing, okay? Can we just not do this?"

"Those are high school boys?" Fiona gasped. The boys dressed all in black like Mariah. "They're not very cute, are they? I thought high school boys were hotter than that."

"It's just Mariah," Madison argued. "She'd be happy to say hello."

"Maddie," Aimee moaned.

"Okay, okay, *fine*," Madison said. As she turned to walk away, Madison looked over once more, only this time Mariah spotted her. She waved. Madison felt her heart leap a little. Mariah *was* a friend—and not just some too-cool freshman. Mariah's boyfriends didn't wave, but that was okay.

"See?" Madison nudged Aimee, who saw the wave, too.

They both waved back. Mariah went back to eating french fries.

"I guess I was wrong," Aimee said sheepishly as they wandered away.

"I guess," Madison said. She didn't want to make Aimee feel bad, even if she *had* been wrong.

"Look over there!" Fiona yelled all of a sudden. She spotted the big sign that read PARTY TOWN. It was a supermarket for cheap Halloween stuff: costumes, makeup, decorations, and props in one-stop shopping.

The first costume they saw was on display at the front of the store. It was a cavewoman outfit. "We probably couldn't wear that at school," Madison said, joking around.

"It would make my butt look big, too, I think." Aimee laughed.

"Your butt!" Fiona laughed. "Aimee, you barely have a butt."

Aimee twisted around to see what her behind looked like. "I do too."

"Yeah, whatever," Madison grumbled. She hated it when Aimee acted fat.

Fiona ran to the back of the store and pulled a grass skirt and green tights from one shelf. She'd decided to borrow one of her mom's Hawaiian short-sleeved shirts and tie it up at the waist. She could wear her braids up, too, with flowers, in her hair. The party store had silk flowers, and she picked out purple, yellow, and coral ones.

Aimee already had most of her ballerina costume at home, so she didn't need to get anything. She found some pink ribbon to wrap into braids and a bun on top of her head.

"This ribbon will totally match my new lipstick shade: Think Pink," Aimee said, admiring the bright color.

Still unable to find a costume, Madison picked through the mask sections, tried on wigs in every length and color, and even put on a Dr. Seuss *Cat in the Hat* hat. It was too big and floppy, though, and kept sliding down her head. Plus it made her think of the first-grade play. She wanted to look older, not younger. She wanted to look like junior high, not elementary school.

Aimee and Fiona bought their stuff, and the three of them went off to meet Mrs. Gillespie at the fountain. Aimee and Fiona opened their bags to show Mrs. Gillespie the costumes. Aimee's mother gave Madison a tight squeeze and whispered, "I'm sure you'll come up with a great costume in no time, Madison."

Madison got quieter than quiet. Was Mrs. Gillespie right? She racked her brain for great costume ideas . . . story ideas . . . over-thinking, as usual.

In the car, Aimee and Fiona were talking about

the stars of the newest teen movie, *Breaking Up Is Easy*, which was showing in the Mall-Plex theater.

"Can we go see that, Mom?" Aimee asked.

"When they change the rating from PG-13, you can," Mrs. Gillespie said with a chuckle. "Either that or when you're thirteen."

Aimee huffed. Sometimes it was such a drag to be twelve and not thirteen.

As they pulled into the Waterses' driveway, Madison twisted her head up and sideways to peer out the car window up at the attic windows. They looked dark and spooky.

Mrs. Waters raved about Fiona's grass skirt and Aimee's ribbons.

Then she put her arm around Madison. "I'm sure you'll think up a great costume, Madison," she said.

Madison smiled, but inside she wondered why everyone kept saying that.

Mrs. Waters made hot chocolate and topped their steaming mugs with squirts of whipped cream. Then the girls moved into the den and sat on a big, comfy couch.

"I like cocoa with those teeny marshmallows more than this," Fiona said. "But my mom got the plain kind. Sorry."

"No biggie." Madison nodded, taking a careful sip.

"I think we should tell ghost stories or something scary," Aimee said, pretending to shudder.

"Yeah." Fiona laughed a little. "Ghosts are okay to talk about. As long as we don't have any in this house."

Madison looked at her friend. "Well, you could."

Fiona looked her squarely in the eye. "What are you talking about, Maddie?"

"Just that . . . well . . . there could be a ghost here," Madison said. "Like in the attic or somewhere."

"Are you for real?" Aimee snorted. She looked like she would fall off the couch.

"I haven't gone up to the attic since we moved into the house," Fiona said.

All of a sudden Aimee jumped off the couch. *"Oh my God!"* she shrieked. "I know who the ghost is! Maddie, remember the people who used to live in this house? You know who I mean!"

Madison hugged her knees to her chest. "You mean the Martins?" she said.

"What are you talking about?" Fiona asked. "What Martins?"

"The Martins were this family who used to live here," Aimee explained. "I used to think their whole story was just a rumor. But maybe *not*!"

"You mean there's really a ghost story about . . ." Fiona took a deep breath. "About this house? *My* house?"

Aimee squealed. "This is *so* cool." The girls huddled closer together, and Madison told the whole story.

"The way the story goes is that the Martin family had this dance party one night and Mrs. Martin came up into the attic to get a ball gown or something. She wanted to look especially beautiful for the dance. Anyway, she was looking around and she went into this big chest, looking for the dress. And she was trying it on and posing in front of the mirror and—"

Madison stopped herself.

"Are you guys sure you want to hear this?" she said.

"Yes, yes, *yes!*" Aimee yelled.

Fiona gulped. "Go on."

"Well, a lot of time passed. The rumor is that Mr. Martin started to get worried about his wife after an hour or so. She hadn't come back downstairs. So he went up to look for her. Up into the attic."

"Into *my* attic?" Fiona said. "You're positive?"

Madison nodded.

"Isn't this the spookiest? I love it!" Aimee said.

"So Mr. Martin went looking for his wife and couldn't find her anywhere. They couldn't figure out what happened. The whole town of Far Hills sent out a search party, and they looked all over the house and neighborhood for his missing wife. They found nothing."

"Tell her the next part, Maddie," Aimee said. "Fiona, the next part is the best—"

"Many years later, Mr. Martin died. Everyone said

he died of a broken heart. So his family moved out of the house. And when they were moving, someone found the old chest. It was sealed shut, but they pried it open and inside . . ."

Fiona covered her ears. "*What?* Don't tell me it was the—"

"Say it!" Aimee cheered.

"Inside the chest was . . . *Mrs. Martin!*" Madison screamed.

Fiona looked absolutely horrified.

"Or her skeleton, anyway. Some people think that Mrs. Martin had tried on the dress and then decided to hide in the trunk to surprise her husband and it closed on her, knocking her unconscious and latching shut. She never regained consciousness. Or even if she had, the chest didn't have a safety latch inside. She was trapped forever. And ever."

Aimee had her hand over her mouth, acting a little dramatic, as usual. "Poor Mrs. Martin stuck in a trunk! Isn't that great!"

Fiona gasped.

"I mean, it's awful . . ." Aimee whispered, "that she died and all that, but—"

"No way!" Fiona said. "This did not happen in our attic."

Madison nodded. "It could be true."

"Let's go look!" Aimee said. "Right now."

83

Chapter 8

"I should have brought my lucky charm bracelet with me tonight. I could use it," Madison said. She was shivering a little. "I think you need a little luck to catch a ghost."

Madison, who was very superstitious, had collected many pieces of "lucky" jewelry so far in her life. She usually wore all her lucky rings (one on each finger), but she had taken some of them off earlier in the day. Tonight she only had on her turquoise ring from a shop in New Mexico, a present from Dad after some business trip; her evil eye ring (not an actual eyeball, but close); and her loopy interlocked silver friendship ring. Aimee had the same one, only she'd lost hers right after they bought them last year.

"Okay, I don't care what you say, we have to stop

talking about this ghost thing right now!" Fiona yelped. She was half giggling, but Madison could tell how spooked Fiona had gotten. "Look, there are no ghosts in my house. My family has been here for like five months and we haven't seen anything or heard anything. You guys are scaring me. Cut it out."

"Let's go sit in the other room," Madison suggested. "We can talk about other stuff."

"You know what? Maybe the ghost is here because of the dance," Aimee said, skipping into the living room. The prospect of what might be hiding in the attic was getting her more excited by the minute. When she got excited, she danced. "I think the ghost is here because Mrs. Martin died during a dance—and we're about to have a dance. You think? That's a pretty strong connection. . . ."

"Gee, that could be true," Madison said aloud. "It makes some kind of sense. And it is Halloween . . ."

"Maddie, this makes *no* sense!" Fiona said. "Ghosts make no sense! They aren't real and there are no ghosts in my house."

"Fiona, don't you think we should just look for Mrs. Martin?" Aimee suggested. "We're all here together tonight. It's perfect! We should go right up to the attic and introduce ourselves."

While Aimee was on a mission to ghost hunt, Fiona was ready to make like a ghost and disappear. Madison had to do something.

"Aimee, why don't we just talk about something

85

else and forget about Mrs. Martin and her dress for a while?" Madison said lightheartedly. "It is Fiona's party."

Aimee looked at Madison and then at Fiona, a little flustered. "I'm sorry. I didn't mean to get so carried away. I promise I won't talk about the ghost anymore."

In a teeny voice Fiona said, "Thanks, Aimee."

The girls brought their hot chocolate mugs to the kitchen for refills and then raced up to Fiona's bedroom. Aimee flopped on the bed and looked over at Fiona's massive Beanie Baby collection. She liked the pink Millennium Bear the best.

Madison scanned Fiona's shelves and yanked down an old yearbook. The cover was red with gold foil, the colors of Fiona's old school in California. Half the pages had the corners turned down and someone had written in Magic Marker on the back cover, *Thanks for a fun year!* Fiona showed them all photographs of her old friends.

"I have to show you guys something else," Fiona said, leaning under her bed to get a huge box. Inside was every copy of *Sports Illustrated for Kids.* She had a plastic folder filled with articles and photos of Mia Hamm, the U.S. women's soccer team star. "She's my idol."

Aimee rolled onto the floor. "Did I tell you that I saw Mrs. Wing and her husband in the school lobby yesterday?" she said.

"What? No!" Fiona giggled. "What does he look like?"

"He's really tall and very cute!" Aimee squealed. "He had on dark glasses."

"I've seen pictures in the computer lab. How tall is he?" Madison asked.

Aimee shrugged. "Tall, tall. And cute. She is soooo lucky."

"Do you really think he's a spy?" Madison asked.

"A spy?" Aimee cracked up. "Where did you hear that one?"

"From you," Madison said, grinning at Aimee.

"Maybe he is," Fiona said. "Maybe he's undercover."

"In Far Hills?" Madison asked.

"*Deep* undercover," Fiona replied.

For a split second Madison considered the idea that Mr. Wing, Spy King, might make a good subject for the bigfishbowl.com story contest. Maybe he was a covert operative for the junior high school confederation, caught in an *international* web . . . of intrigue!

Aimee's stomach grumbled and the friends burst into laughter.

"Let's get another snack," Fiona said. The girls headed back into the kitchen for microwave popcorn.

"I still can't stop thinking about poor Mrs. Martin," Aimee said in a low voice. "How claustrophobic."

Fiona, who was sitting on the edge of the counter, threw a dishtowel at Aimee.

"Hey!" Aimee said. "What was that for?"

"I told you not to bring up the ghost!" Fiona said. "Mentioning a ghost on the way home from school or even in the middle of a dark graveyard is okay. But talking about one above my bedroom isn't."

"Aimee, you promised!" Madison said.

"I know! I'm sorry. I won't talk about her," Aimee said. "But the thing is . . . What if we have a séance and see if the ghost answers? Then we'll know if Mrs. Martin is really here."

"Now?" Fiona said. "A séance?"

"Let's do something other than sit around and eat," Aimee said. "Come on, Fiona, don't be scared. We'll all be there."

"Can't we just talk about boys and other people from school instead?" Fiona asked.

"How about Ivy? She's pretty scary, isn't she?" Madison chuckled.

"No! You have to do this séance with me," Aimee said. "Let's go into the bathroom."

"What?" Madison laughed. "The bathroom? Aimee, you're crazy."

"I'm serious," Aimee said. "I told you ghosts are *serious*. Let's go into the hall bathroom. Is that okay, Fiona?"

She nodded reluctantly, and the three of them

squeezed in and shut the door. Madison turned the lights down real low.

"Maddie, you have to turn out the lights *completely* or it doesn't work," Aimee said.

The small bathroom went black except for the hall light glowing under the bottom of the bathroom door.

"This is so freaky," Madison said. "Now *I'm* scared."

"Do we have to do this in the *dark*?" Fiona's voice was barely audible.

"Here's what we have to do. Face the mirror together. Then we'll see it," Aimee said. As their eyes slowly adjusted to the dark, murky reflections appeared before them.

"See what?" Madison asked.

"The ghost. Look, I did this with my brother Billy once. Just wait and watch," Aimee tried to assure them.

A minute went by.

And then another minute after that. It was getting warm.

Brrrrrrrrrrreeeeeeeeeeep!

Fiona's digital watch beeped. The noise almost sent the trio crashing into the shower.

"Whoa!" Aimee screamed.

"What?" Fiona and Madison said at the same time.

"Look! Did you see that?" Aimee asked, pointing at the mirror. "Look! *That*."

"What?" Madison said, looking closer. "Is it Mrs. Martin?"

"I have such a bad feeling about this," Fiona said.

There was a knock at the door and all three girls screamed at once.

"What are you doing in there?" a voice said from the hallway. "Is everyone all right?"

Aimee clicked on the bathroom light and the room glowed white.

Fiona turned the knob and opened the door. It wasn't Mrs. Martin. It was Mrs. Waters.

"Mom!" Fiona cried. She grabbed her mother's arm.

"Fiona?" Mrs. Waters said. "Why were you three in the bathroom together in the dark? Is something wrong?"

Aimee and Madison started giggling. They couldn't help themselves.

"Why on earth would you girls lock yourselves in a bathroom?" Mrs. Waters asked again. "You could have gotten hurt with all of you stuck inside here like this."

"Mrs. Waters, do you believe in ghosts?" Aimee asked the question no one else had the nerve to ask.

Mrs. Waters thought for a moment. "Well, I don't know, Aimee. Depends on my mood. If I were in a deserted old castle, maybe. Right now, *no*."

"Mom, have you ever been up to our attic?" Fiona asked.

Mrs. Waters shook her head. "Only once or twice. It's mostly empty. Why do you ask? Do we have ghosts living up there?"

"Well . . ." Fiona started to say.

"Madison and I think there is a high probability and likelihood that ghosts are here at your house," Aimee said. She sounded like one of those TV investigators.

"Mrs. Waters, did you said the attic is *mostly* empty?" Madison asked. "What do you mean by 'mostly'?"

"Mostly empty except for a few boxes and pipes . . . and there's an old chest. . . ."

"*Aaaaaaaaaaaaaaaaaaaaaaaaaaaaaah!*" all three girls screamed at once—*again.*

"*Girls!*" Mrs. Waters covered her ears. "Stop that screaming."

"We have to go check it out for ourselves!" Aimee shrieked. She asked Mrs. Waters nicely. "Can we go up into the attic? Can we? Can we?"

"Aimee, I really don't think you girls should be going up there exploring. I don't know how safe it is. And besides . . ."

"Please, Mom." Fiona spoke up. She wasn't sure she really wanted to come face-to-face with a ghost, but she also didn't want to spend the rest of the night imagining what *might* be up there.

Mrs. Waters still wasn't sure. "I just don't know, dear."

Aimee started pleading again. "We—but—Mrs. Waters—please—"

She could be very convincing when she wrinkled up her face and opened her eyes as wide as quarters. Madison thought the whole thing was pretty funny.

"Mommy, it's a matter of life or death," Fiona said.

"Life or *death*?" Mrs. Waters gasped, laughing. "Fiona Jane Waters, don't be ridiculous."

Madison finally butted in. "Mrs. Waters, there really could be a ghost up there. You see, there's an old neighborhood legend about the attic in this house. . . ." Madison explained the whole thing all over again.

"You girls have some imaginations," Mrs. Waters said. "I supposed I should be impressed. Old attics usually have a lot of secrets—but ghosts?"

"Please," Fiona begged one last time.

"Well . . . I don't think you'll find much of anything, but . . . okay. Okay, you can go up there. Do you three promise me you will be careful?"

They all nodded.

"Let me go get the big flashlight, then." Mrs. Waters disappeared out the door.

For some reason they were still all standing in the teeny bathroom, which now felt even more cramped and hotter than before.

Fiona sighed. "Let's go back to my bedroom and make a plan."

"I bet this wasn't what you had in mind when you invited us over," Aimee joked.

"Yeah. I thought we'd be painting our toenails by now," Madison said.

"We can do that stuff later," Aimee said. "This is better. Isn't it? I'm so glad your mom said yes."

"This is fun," Madison said. "I can't believe we actually told the truth about the ghost. I thought it would make her more worried."

"She doesn't believe in ghosts," Fiona said. "She watches sci-fi movies all the time and never gets scared. Besides, even if Mrs. Martin came out, she could probably kick her butt."

Madison laughed. "Well, that's good, I guess."

"I told you ghosts could be anywhere, right?" Aimee said. "And now we're going to see a real, live one. Right here in this house."

Chapter 9

The stairway up to the Waterses' attic didn't seem old or scary at all. Someone had redone the steps, so it wasn't too treacherous to climb. Madison led the way, followed by Aimee and then Fiona.

"This isn't so scary," Aimee said as she stepped up.

"Speak for yourself, Aim," Fiona said.

"We'll have great stories to tell at the school dance next week, won't we?" Madison said. She reached the top of the pull-down wooden stairs and poked her head up first.

"Wow," Madison said, finally reaching the attic space. Her friends climbed in after her. They all looked around and saw an enormous chest.

"Oh my God!" Aimee screamed. "Mrs. Martin!"

94

"Girls!" Mrs. Waters called up to them from downstairs. "I don't want you up there too long, make it quick!"

Madison poked her head through the opening just a little bit. "We're only going to be here for a split second, I promise, Mrs. Waters. Right down after that."

The friends walked over to where the chest had been shoved into place. It was obvious no one had moved it for ages. It was a big sea chest with chains and buckles on it.

"Maddie, it looks like the one you described in the story," Aimee said.

"And it's big enough for a person." Fiona gulped.

The chest was enormous and covered in dust, nicks, cobwebs, scratches, dents, and other signs of a long, long life. On the side were carved the initials F.D.M. Everyone seemed to recognize what the letter *M* stood for.

Martin.

"This is crazy," Aimee said, a little breathless.

After a moment, their eyes adjusted to the darkness some more. Fiona found a single lightbulb cord and pulled. The whole room lit up. The chest and the rest of the attic were covered in an inch-thick layer of dust.

"Madison!" Aimee cried out when the room brightened. "Watch out!"

Madison felt something on her face. Something sticky. She was snarled in a thick spiderweb.

"How disgusting," Fiona said, trying to peel pieces of web off Madison's shirt and hair.

"Grosser than gross," Madison groaned. She'd have to reconsider her love of spiders and all things creepy-crawly after this.

"Let's go back downstairs," Fiona said, turning away. "We saw the chest. The ghost isn't around. Okay?"

"We haven't even opened it!" Aimee said.

"You guys seem to forget one very important thing," Fiona said. "I live here."

"Isn't that a better reason for wanting to see what's in this?" Madison asked. "Just in case . . ."

"In case *what*?" Fiona asked.

Aimee was already kneeling down, trying to open the latch. "Drat," she wailed. "It's locked."

"I'm going back downstairs." Fiona turned again to walk away from her friends. "I don't wanna see this Martin lady or anything else that's inside that chest. I'm going back to have another cup of hot chocolate even if it doesn't have little baby marsh-mallows in it."

Aimee struggled with the bolt. "Dean showed me once how to pick a lock."

"Really?" Fiona stopped short, incredulous. "Your brother picks locks?"

"Whatever," Aimee said. She took a clip from

her hair and worked the lock. "They do this on TV."

Fiona looked at Madison. Madison shrugged. Aimee liked to exaggerate, but she really seemed to know what she was doing.

"Try this," Fiona said, handing her a piece of scraggly metal from the floor of the attic.

"Weren't you leaving?" Madison asked.

"Maybe," Fiona shrugged and stayed put.

"Is this against the law? I mean, opening some-one else's chest?" Madison asked.

"Got it!" Aimee smiled and tossed the metal piece aside. Madison was shocked. Upon closer inspection Madison noticed that the lock had not, in fact, been picked. The whole contraption was rusted and had broken open.

"Now, everyone, on the count of three," Aimee said. "We'll open it together."

"One . . ."

"Two . . ."

"Three!" Madison sneezed on the count. There was a lot of dust up in this attic. The lid popped open. Fiona shrieked.

"Oh my God!" Aimee yelled.

It was empty.

"What a gyp!" Aimee yelled again.

"Where did Mrs. Martin go?" Madison asked aloud.

Fiona looked all around them. "Did she fly out, maybe? Ghosts do that, don't they?"

"She's a sneaky one, that ghost," Madison teased.

"Was she even here?" Aimee asked. "I mean, come on."

"What did we really expect to see?" Madison asked. "A skeleton?"

Fiona shuddered. "She's still here. I bet she's watching us. Right now . . ."

"Girls!" Fiona's mother called from downstairs.

"Ahhhhh!" This time Aimee was the one who jumped.

"Did someone fall? I thought I heard a loud noise. Girls?"

Aimee clutched her chest. "It's just your mother."

Madison started to laugh. They all did.

"Don't worry, Mom." Fiona giggled. "Don't worry. We're just—"

"Scaring ourselves silly," Aimee said.

They all climbed back downstairs, giggling all the way. "Dinner is ready, girls," Mrs. Waters said. She closed the attic door and hustled the friends into the kitchen.

After dinner the trio headed back into Fiona's bedroom. Aimee offered to French-braid Madison's hair, and Fiona tried her new Frosted Grape nail polish.

"Maybe instead of a hula dancer I should go as a witch to the school dance," Fiona said. "I could put white in my black hair. Something to look weird. It gets all frizzy when I let my braids out."

"It looks so cool down," Aimee said.

"A little nappy," Fiona said, "but I like it this way."

Fiona looked so good all the time—and even more with her hair down. Madison figured that every seventh-grade boy would be asking her to dance next week. Fiona was a perfect combination of pretty and smart and athletic.

"So where's Chet tonight?" Aimee asked.

Fiona explained that Chet was staying over at Hart's house with Egg and Drew. Madison wondered what they were doing. Were they talking about *girls*?

"It's like *Night of the Twin Sleepovers*," Madison joked.

"*Night at Haunted House*, you mean," Aimee added.

Fiona grimaced. "No more ghosts!" She sat back to admire her perfectly painted toes.

"Is Chet going to the dance?" Madison asked, putting some Frosted Grape on her own toes.

Fiona shrugged. "Probably. But he won't dance or anything. Chet's scared of girls. He likes to act cool, but he's a real chicken."

"I've never danced with a boy," Madison admitted aloud.

"Really?" Fiona said.

Aimee got quiet all of a sudden. "Me neither," she said.

99

"What are you talking about?" Madison said. "All you do is dance."

"Not the kind we're talking about, though. Not real dancing. Not with a real boy that I like or anything. What about you, Fiona?"

She shrugged. "Yeah, I had a boyfriend in California and we—"

Squeeeeeeeeeak.

"What was that?" Madison asked. "Did you guys hear that? Right above us?"

Fiona, who'd been sitting sprawled on her own bed, grabbed a pillow and pushed herself up against the wall. "I don't know. Did you hear it?"

Squeeeeeeeeeak.

"Heard it," Aimee said as the noise repeated itself. "Twice."

"It's Ma-Ma-Mrs. Martin!" Fiona stuttered, scared.

"No way!" Madison said. *"No way."*

The three girls dove under the quilt on top of Fiona's bed and vowed never to come out until they had a surefire plan on how to deal with the situation.

"It could just be the floor up there," Madison said.

"Yeah, with the sound of a ghost walking on it!" Aimee said.

"Isn't there any nice way we can ask her to leave my house?" Fiona said.

"Wait! Did you bring the Ouija board, Aimee? That might work," Madison suggested.

"You really want to try talking to this ghost again?" Fiona cried.

"Yes!" Aimee said. She bounded off to get the Ouija board from her overnight bag.

Fiona's room was covered with a plush green carpet. The trio sat down on it like they were setting up some kind of ghost picnic.

"Now, you have to take this seriously," Aimee warned the other two as she opened the box and the board. "No laughing in the middle of it like before."

"Who's laughing?" Madison said, checking out the plastic pointer. Aimee called it the planchette, but to Madison it looked like the little plastic holder found in the center of a takeout pizza.

"Hey, Maddie." Fiona leaned over and picked a string off Madison's shirt. "You still have spiderweb on you. Which is now probably on my bed, thank you very much."

"Sorry," Madison said. "Okay, what question do we wanna ask?"

Aimee clucked her tongue. "We want to ask about Mrs. Martin. Why is she here? Something like that. We want to know about the ghost."

The Ouija "Mystifying Oracle" board looked ominous. It was a special edition that Aimee's mother bought. At the upper-left corner was the word *yes*.

In the upper-right corner was the word *no*. At the center were all the letters of the alphabet, the numerals one through nine, and then on the bottom were two more words: *good* and *bye*. Aimee turned the lights down lower and the board glowed.

"Again with the lights?" Fiona said. "Jeepers."

"Let's start with something simple," Aimee suggested, putting her fingertips on the pointer. "I'll ask. 'Will I be a dancer when I grow up?'"

"That's the question we're asking?" Madison asked, incredulous.

"For now. Like a test."

Fiona giggled. "What does your dancing have to do with ghosts, Aimee?"

"Okay, fine. You ask the question, then." Aimee backed away from the board. She handed the planchette to Madison.

"We need to concentrate," Madison suggested.

"I thought you always made fun of this stuff," Aimee said.

"That was before I saw Fiona's attic," Madison said.

The three girls closed their eyes tightly and placed the pointer back onto the Ouija board.

"Is Mrs. Martin in this house?" Madison asked.

Fiona freaked out as their fingers moved across the board. The planchette pointed to *yes*.

"Did you guys press it that way on purpose?" she asked.

Madison and Aimee shook their heads no.

"Is Mrs. Martin unhappy?" Aimee asked.

The second answer was *no*.

"Well, is she haunting my house?" Fiona asked.

The third question spelled something out very slowly.

"*M-a-c-h-k-l?*" Fiona asked. "What's that supposed to be?"

"The first two letters are *ma* like Martin," Madison said.

"The last two letters look like *kl*. It could be like kill," Aimee said. "Maybe Mrs. Martin is trying to tell us that she was killed."

"So then what's *ch* for?" Fiona said. "Chocolate? Hot chocolate!"

They all laughed and collapsed onto the carpet. Aimee put the game away. Even ghost hunts could get boring.

"Hey, let's go online," Fiona suggested.

They went back downstairs into the den to log on to the computer. Fiona booted up the computer and logged on to bigfishbowl.com.

On-screen, skeleton fish were swimming around inside the home page fishbowl with little bubbles over their fish heads: BOO! OOH! NOO! They looked so cute. Aimee started pointing and naming them after horror movie characters like Dracula and Swamp Thing. She called one "The Wolf-Fish."

At the top of the home page was the banner

invitation to enter the Caught in the Web contest. There was a countdown clock in a sidebar to show the deadline fast approaching. Madison bit her lip. With all the ghostly excitement, she'd nearly forgotten about the contest.

She had to come up with an idea for her story!

Fiona didn't pay attention to all the flashing stuff at the top of the page. She ignored the contest and skipped right over the skeleton fish—clicking into a chat area called "Girls Only." Madison caught her breath when she saw the roster of members chatting there.

Bigwheels was at the top of the list.

Madison couldn't believe it. She'd already lied to Aimee about her keypal once. She didn't want to have to do it again. Did Aimee recognize the name? Would she ask about it?

Zzzzzzzzzzap!

Suddenly the room flashed and then went black. *Bigwheels* and everything else on-screen was gone. It got so quiet. The chugging sound of the refrigerator had turned off with everything else.

"Fiona, your computer exploded," Aimee said, sitting there in the dark.

"I think the power just blew. Like in the wires or something," Fiona said. "It usually only happens during a thunderstorm."

"That's weird," Madison said. "It's not raining out."

"Girls!" It didn't long for Mrs. Waters to come into the kitchen with the enormous flashlight. She lit some candles on the counter. "Is everyone okay in here?"

"The computer just went poof, Mrs. Waters," Aimee said.

"So weird," Madison said again.

"Mommy, what happened?" Fiona asked.

"It's just an old house. I have to flip the circuit breakers down in the basement. I'll be right back. Will you girls be okay up here without me?"

"We're okay as long as Mrs. Martin doesn't come back," Fiona said.

"Who?" Mrs. Waters asked. "Who's Mrs. Martin?"

"A friend," Madison said.

The three friends looked at each other and smiled.

"I see," Mrs. Waters said, walking toward the basement stairs. As she turned around, her eyes lit up with candlelight. She looked like a character from a horror movie going off to the dungeon.

"Don't worry about us," Aimee called after her, laughing nervously. "We'll be right here. Unless we see a . . ."

Fiona punched her jokingly. "Nooooo! The minute the power goes back on, we're doing beauty stuff. *No more ghosts.*"

"Okay! And we'll have a pillow fight, too." Aimee fake-punched her back.

Madison held up her hands and stretched them out to make shapes from shadows on the wall. She used her thumb and the rest of her fingers to make a "duck" quack its bill open and shut. Aimee made a bird flap its wings.

Three minutes later, the power kicked back in and everything in the kitchen surged on at once. The refrigerator hummed. Everyone cheered. Mrs. Waters came back upstairs.

Madison felt a surge, too—inside herself.

Thanks to Mrs. Martin and her best friends and the power outage, she suddenly had the most wonderful, frightful idea.

It was an idea that just might win her the Caught in the Web contest.

Chapter 10

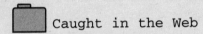 Caught in the Web

Rude Awakening: You can do *anything* once the ghost is clear.

Just sent in my story. Fingers crossed. I hope I win!

Aimee said the story is superscary, and she's pretty much of a ghost expert, especially after our sleepover at Fiona's house.

Fiona, of course, won't read the story. She says it's so close to the truth. That scares her. I don't really mind. But I will make her read it if I win, that's for sure.

Mom liked it, too, a lot. She says I should mail one to Gramma Helen. I need to send it to Dad and Bigwheels, too. Still

haven't told Aimee about my keypal yet.
I'll do it soon.

Madison attached a copy of the story to her file. She printed out one to mail to Gramma.

The Secret of the Old Trunk
by MadFinn@bigfishbowl.com
*IT WAS A DARK AND STORMY NIGHT. THE HOUSE
WAS DEAD QUIET, EXCEPT FOR* the sound of leaves
and rain on the roof. An old man stared at a
picture on the wall. It was his wife. Her name
was Ivy. Ivy had disappeared many years before.
She had gone up to the attic before her wedding
day to get an old blue dress in an old trunk.
That was what she said. But she never returned.
Her husband-to-be looked everywhere for her but
found nothing. He didn't look in the chest,
though. It was sealed shut.
    Years went by.
    One summer, the man's niece came to stay with
him. Her name was Ivy, after the aunt she never
knew. She found a photo album with pictures of
Ivy and asked a lot of questions. The old man
didn't like her being so nosy. She asked if
she could go into the attic one day, and he
said no, it was off-limits. But she went anyway.
    When she got up there, she saw a trunk. It
was very late at night, so she tried to be as
quiet as a mouse. She had a skeleton key in
her pocket to open the trunk. It worked and
the lid cracked open.
    There was an awful, terrible smell. She

108

raised the lid a little more. Then she heard footsteps behind her.

"Go ahead and open it," the voice said. She knew it was the old man. He said, "Open it," three times.

She trembled and quaked.

"I SAID, OPEN IT!" the man screamed at her.

The girl pushed open the lid, covering her nose and eyes as she did. She gasped with fear.

"Look inside," the man said.

And so the girl did. She leaned over and peered in.

"OH!" the girl screamed when she saw what was inside.

It was a blue dress!

The man put his hand on his niece's shoulder and squeezed tight.

"I keep this here," the man said in a low voice. "In case my dear Ivy wants to wear it . . . to her GHOST ball!"

"Maddie!" Mom called from downstairs all of a sudden. "Telephone!"

Madison closed the file and went to get the call. Dad wanted to know if Saturday's sleepover had been a success. Madison told him about the power outage, the ghost, the Ouija board, *and* being scared silly.

"Hey, Maddie, what happened to the ghost who went to a school dance?" Dad asked on the phone.

"I don't know, Dad. *What?*" Madison said.

"It had a *wail* of a time!" Dad chuckled.

"Daaaaad!" Madison was the one wailing.

"Do you have a costume for Friday's dance yet?" he asked.

"No," Madison moaned. "Aimee's going to be a ballerina, Fiona's a hula girl. Everyone else's costumes are so cool."

"I'll bet your mother can help you think of something. Why don't you ask her?" Dad said.

"I want to do this myself," Madison said.

After hanging up, Madison dragged herself back upstairs into her closet. She had to start thinking now. Was there a costume hiding inside? She thought about dressing like a hobo, but that wouldn't be original enough. Online she'd seen a T-shirt with a Halloween message that read: THIS IS MY HALLOWEEN COSTUME. Madison thought making a shirt like that would be hysterical, but it wasn't creative enough for a dance.

She went to check out Mom's closet. A blue dress in the corner caught her eye. She could go as Mrs. Martin! But being an invisible ghost wasn't such a great idea for the dance either. She needed people to notice her—especially people like Hart.

Then a caftan dress from a trip to Greece caught Madison's attention. It was a little big, but Madison liked the way it looked. It was a burnt orange color. She tried it on over her jeans.

Mom loved the dress and said Madison could use some other props to go with it for a costume.

110

Madison thought about who she was dressing up to be. She remembered reading *D'Aulaires' Book of Greek Myths* from school. She loved Greek heroes and heroines. Madison decided she would be Aphrodite, goddess of love. She didn't want to be a ballerina or hula girl or anything that would be perceived as ordinary. Besides, dressing up as a goddess of love meant her odds for capturing Hart's attention were probably increased.

Not that she had a clue what to do if she ever *did* get him to notice her.

There were still four more days left before the dance, which meant four more days of worrying. But school got busier than busy that week for Madison.

It was the end of marking period and teachers were tallying first-term reports. This meant they were also giving quizzes and tests and essays and *everything* else. Madison had to spend more time on homework and less time on files and ghost hunts. She'd clocked in some extra time with Mrs. Wing and the school Web site, too.

Fiona was super busy, too. The Rangers had won each of their district play-off games. Now they were the team to beat in the entire league. Fiona was happy about it, but all the time devoted to soccer meant less time for Halloween dance committee meetings.

Madison missed seeing Fiona at meetings. Aimee

had even missed one afternoon because of dance practice.

Even when Fiona and Aimee were there, they were busy planning for the food or music. Madison had to decorate the gymnasium and cafeteria alone alongside Poison Ivy. And the enemy was as bossy as ever.

"What are *you* doing?" Ivy asked Madison, waltzing over with her hands on her hips. She was wearing a short green dress that looked like tie-dye and clunky black shoes, looking as perfect as ever. She'd been putting up balloons across the back wall.

Madison looked down at the giant package of gauzy web material she was holding. She'd been given the responsibility today of hanging it from the ceiling to the floor in one corner of the room. She had to make a spider's web. Her brain buzzed with the idea that maybe, just like in *Charlotte's Web*, she could stretch the gauze so the web had an actual word at its center. Madison imagined a fake web with the word *DANCE* inside.

"Uh . . . I'm making a spider's web," Madison said. "And I have black construction paper spiders and other bugs to put in the middle."

"Oh, *really*?" Ivy snickered. "Well, I guess it looks like a web."

"What are you doing?" Madison asked.

"I put up signs for the bathrooms and balloons and other things," Ivy said. "Let me see that Web stuff that you're doing."

Madison couldn't believe that Ivy's motives for helping were good ones, but she agreed to let her help with the web. Working together, they could get the gauze stretched out in half the time.

"Why don't you attach it up to the wall there?" Ivy pointed. "I'll hang on to the gauze here." They'd only been at it a few moments, and already Ivy was up to her old tricks.

But Madison agreed it was a good idea, so she leaned over toward the wall. She stretched up with some of the gauze and stretched and . . .

Ooops!

Madison fell right into the wall. Even worse, she fell right into the gauze, causing it to detach. A big piece floated to the floor. She was wrapped in webbing and she couldn't get out.

Ivy roared. She almost looked like she'd turn purple, she was laughing so hard. Soon enough, everyone else heard, too, and they dashed over to see what was the matter. Even Señora Diaz was laughing a little bit as she helped detach Madison from the webbing. Aimee and Egg rushed over from the kitchen and covered their mouths so they wouldn't explode with laughter, too.

"*Oh!*" Aimee cried. "Are you okay Maddie?"

Madison wasn't laughing *at all*. She looked at everyone's faces, including her best friends'. Her stomach went flip-flop. She wanted to run.

But she was caught in the web.

Chapter 11

"Let me see you!" Mom cried. She snapped pictures of Madison in her costume from all angles. "Oh, I'm so happy that you thought of this outfit."

Mom had called up another one of her buddies from Budge Films, where she worked, and arranged to borrow a scepter from the props department. It was made of papier mâché, so it was light enough to carry. Madison made a crown from tinfoil that she spray-painted gold with Mom's help. She also found some junk jewelry in a drawer in Mom's room.

"You look like a real goddess, honey bear," Mom said. She put down the camera so she could adjust Madison's up 'do. Little ringlets fell down her blushed cheeks.

"Oh, Mom." Madison sighed. "Please just take the picture."

"Just stand still, Aphrodite." Dad spoke up. He was standing in the hallway, waiting to drive Madison over to the Halloween dance.

"Thank you, Jeff, for being here," Mom said.

Madison felt weird hearing Mom say Dad's name nicely like that. All three of the Finns were back in the Finn living room together. It was like old times; even Phinnie could tell the difference. The pug was chasing his little curlicue tail and snorting. Dad picked up the dog to calm him down, but Phin wriggled right out of Dad's grip.

Moments later, after several more pictures and kisses and oohs and ahhs, Madison and Dad were in the car. She took a mental inventory: scepter, crown, lip gloss. . . .

The dance started in twenty minutes.

Now that she was all dressed up, she wanted to stay looking pretty during the dance. Would boys notice her—especially one boy in particular? It was Madison's first *real* dance, and she just wanted to be there already! The anticipation made her dizzy. Madison barely said two more words to Dad the whole drive over.

The Far Hills Junior High School parking lot was a madhouse.

One kid dressed up as a giant eyeball in a tuxedo almost fell over and someone had to lead him into the main doors. Madison saw witches, werewolves, and about four ninjas. Egg would be mad about that. He was hoping to be one of a kind. There were hockey players, ghosts, and pop singers. One group of friends had all dressed like an alien family.

Even teachers and chaperones were costumed. Madison chuckled when she saw her substitute science teacher show up as none other than Frankenstein himself—bolts and all.

"Have a great time," Dad said, leaning out the window of the car to kiss his daughter good-bye.

"Okay, Dad." Madison waved him off. "Okay. Bye."

"We'll have dinner when I get back from Boston."

"Okay, Dad," Madison repeated, backing away from his car. "Have a nice trip."

Madison stumbled up the curb. She was the one having the nice trip.

"Be careful," Dad said, pulling away. "And don't forget to have fun!"

Madison wiggled inside her caftan and adjusted her crown. She took a deep breath and walked carefully into the school lobby.

"You're here!" Aimee squealed. She twirled over in her ballerina outfit, followed by her brother Roger.

"You look sooooo good," Aimee said. "Who did your hair like that?"

"Mom," Madison mumbled. "You look good, too. Where's Fiona?"

"She's not here yet," Aimee said.

"Hey, Roger," Madison said to Aimee's brother. "You're a chaperone?"

"Yup. That's me. You've got a nice costume," he added. "Roman goddess of the Halloween dance, eh?"

Madison blushed under her blush. Roger smiled back.

"Hello, all," Fiona said, walking in the front door. She had on a Hawaiian shirt plus a grass skirt and about ten plastic leis around her neck. Chet was standing behind her on the way in, but he didn't stick around. He just stuck his hand up for a quick wave and dashed into the gym.

"Who's Chet supposed to be?" Aimee asked.

"A martian." Fiona laughed. "What else? Didn't you see those little bobbling antenna things on his head?"

The school had a security guard posted at the doorway to the school and again to the cafeteria and gym. They wanted to be careful to check students' bags to make sure no one brought anything inside they weren't supposed to bring.

Madison (a.k.a. Aphrodite), Aimee (a.k.a. Ballerina), and Fiona (a.k.a. Hula Girl) approached the doors to the gym, bristling with excitement. Over by the music booth, Madison saw Mrs. Wing dressed for a masquerade ball. She wore a purple dress and a paper mask that just covered her eyes with purple feathers. Standing next to Mrs. Wing was a man in a rubber mask and doctor's scrubs. Madison assumed he was Mr. Wing.

"This is one of my students," she said to her husband as Madison walked over. "This is Madison Finn and—you're Fiona and Aimee, right? I'd like you to meet my husband, Dr. Bryan Wing."

"Who are you supposed to be?" Aimee asked Dr. Wing.

Everyone laughed when he said, "Wolf-Doctor."

"Have a nice time tonight, Madison," Mrs. Wing said. "See you around."

"All our decorations look so cool," Aimee said, whirling in her ballet slippers as they walked into the main part of the gymnasium. "The balloons look good, and that web in the corner really came out nice, Maddie."

"Yeah, even though I fell in it," Madison grumbled.

"It's Egg and Drew!" Fiona pointed across the gym. Egg was in his best ninja gear. Drew had on jeans and a Mets baseball shirt.

"You call that a real costume?" Aimee said to Drew.

"Sure. I'm a Met," Drew replied. "Hey, Maddie. Nice costume."

"Who are you, Maddie?" Egg asked. "Queen of the World?"

"Shut up, Egg. You're only like the tenth ninja I've seen tonight," Madison said.

Madison noticed that he seemed unusually interested in Fiona's grass skirt. "Can you see through
that thing?" he asked her. Fiona giggled.

Aimee rolled her eyes at Madison and whispered,
"He's such a geek sometimes."

"*Hart!*" Drew yelled across the gym to his cousin.
"*Over here!*"

Madison felt her legs get weak. *Hart?* He was on
his way over.

"Yo!" Hart gave all the guys high fives. He was
dressed up like a wizard, just like he said he would
be. He looked even better than he had looked when
he played the Wizard in *The Wiz* at school.

Hart told Aimee he liked her costume, and she
twirled around for him. He smiled at Madison, too,
but didn't say anything more than, "Hey, Finnster,"
just like always. He got distracted when some ninth-
grade DJ turned on the music.

"I'm hungry," Hart said.

"Yeah, let's go check out the food," Egg said.

"See you guys later," Drew said. The boys walked
away together toward the snack table.

Madison clutched her papier-mâché scepter
tight. Hart hadn't said anything about *her* costume.
She had this weird, empty feeling inside. Everyone
else said she looked beautiful. Why hadn't *he*
noticed?

"Let's go dance." Fiona goofed around, moving
her hula-skirted hips to the music.

Aimee grabbed her arm. "We can't dance *yet*. It's too early."

"What?" Madison said. "Who says it's too early?"

"Trust me, it is. Let's just stand here for a while. See? Kids are still walking in. You have to act mellow at first. Then you dance."

Madison usually didn't question Aimee's logic on such matters.

"Look!" Aimee blurted. She was staring at the door to the gym.

Poison Ivy Daly walked through. She had on a red leotard, red tights, red skirt, red shoes, and red scarf, and she had attached a red tail to her behind and red horns to her head.

"She's a devil!" Aimee snorted. "No way. I can't believe she would come dressed like that."

"Me neither," Fiona said, slack jawed.

Madison *could* believe it. The leotard and tights accentuated Ivy's thin body, and everyone stared. She was followed into the room by her drones, Rose and Joanie, who had on boring outfits and too much makeup. They were supposed to be backup singers, according to Aimee. She'd heard them talking about their costumes the day before.

Ivy scanned the room, but she didn't see Madison, Aimee, or Fiona. She did, however, see Hart right away and walked toward the food table.

Madison watched her parade across the Halloween dance floor along with every boy in the room—even eighth and ninth graders. All eyes were on her, just the way Ivy wanted it.

"Just forget her, Maddie. Let's stand in the center of the room," Aimee suggested.

From the center of the room, Madison had a better view of the food table and Hart. She saw Ivy standing near him. At one point he even reached up and touched the horns on the top of her head. No one was really dancing yet, either, just like Aimee had said. There was an unspoken code about what to do and not to do here. Every moment counted.

Eat. Talk. Be seen.

Dance later.

Madison saw another one of her friends from class, Lindsay Frost, across the room. Lindsay was dressed all in black and was holding her mask by her side. She'd come to the dance as a gorilla. Madison wanted to go say hello, but for some reason she didn't. Lindsay was over near the wall, talking to some boys Madison didn't really know too well.

Girls and boys were segregated everywhere you looked, chatting among themselves. Kids were split into cliques and grades. Madison didn't even recognize half the people in the room. Of course, almost everyone was in costume.

Aimee's brother Roger had been right. This was initiation night. Big time.

"Attention, please," a voice crackled over the loudspeaker. "Welcome to the Halloween dance."

One boy made a fart noise and some other boys cheered.

Señora Diaz stood up on the podium. She was the voice behind the microphone. Madison couldn't see Egg from where she was standing, but she imagined he was squirming in his shoes right about now. He got so embarrassed whenever he and his mother were at the same school events.

"As you know," Señora continued, "we have lots of activities going on this evening. And many helpful people here making sure the dance goes well. Please give a round of applause for your family and teachers who have come out to help us tonight—dressed in costumes, no less."

Kids in the room clapped loudly.

"And to the seventh-grade students on the dance committee who helped with the very important decoration and food and music. Let's give them a round of applause. . . ."

Someone whistled. The clapping got louder. Even the eighth and ninth graders were clapping thank-you.

"*Gracias!*" Señora's voice continued. "Now, we have a line forming for the scary hallway at the far end of the gym. If possible, let's keep the screaming contained to that area tonight, *sí*? We'd like everyone to have a chance inside at least once, so please don't get out and get right back on line. Finally, some eighth and ninth graders will be judging seventh graders in a costume contest throughout the night. Everyone have a *great time*!"

The clapping started up again. So did the music.

"I love this song!" Aimee shrieked. It was hip-hop. She started bending and twisting her body to the music.

"Aimee, you said not to dance yet," Madison said.

"Yeah, but that was like ten minutes ago. It's fine now."

"Yeah!" Fiona shrugged and swiveled in her grass skirt again.

Music pounded over the speakers. A few teachers grimaced at the noise, but it kept right on blaring.

Madison bounced up and down, up and down, from her knees only. She couldn't do much more since the caftan didn't allow for a lot of movement. She straightened out her crown and waved her arm into the air once in a while.

Just like that, Aphrodite was dancing.

Chapter 12

Chet ran over to Fiona on the dance floor, whispering something. He was laughing hysterically. Fiona motioned to Aimee and Madison to walk over to the food table.

"Chet says Tommy Kwong put something in the food," Fiona said. "Let's go see for ourselves."

Floating in the giant fruit punch bowl were plastic flies. Even funnier than the floating flies was the fact that Tommy himself was dressed up like some kind of a bug, wearing a hat with pipe-cleaner and pom-pom antennae on top.

"Hey, Finnster!" Hart came up from behind and nearly scared the crown off Madison. "What's up?"

"Oh! Hart, hey," Madison said. She turned sideways in the caftan and almost lost her balance. "Whoa!"

Hart grabbed her elbow.

"Thanks. This dress is so long, you know, it's hard to . . ." Madison's voice drifted off.

"Cool costume. Who are you supposed to be?" Hart asked, adjusting his own wizard cap.

"Um . . . well . . ." Madison thought for a moment. He'd noticed her outfit finally, but she couldn't very well tell the crush of her life that she was Aphrodite, goddess of love. And she didn't have a backup answer.

"I know!" Hart suddenly said. "You're like a walking Greek myth."

"Well, I'm a Roman or Greek mythical character," Madison said politely. "Take your pick."

"Hercules!" he joked.

"Umm . . . I don't think so," Madison said.

"What's that thing?" Hart pointed to her neck.

Madison reached up and felt her neck. She was sweating. A bead of sweat was trickling down her back. Of course, Hart hadn't been pointing to sweat. He was talking about her necklace.

"Is it real gold?" he asked.

Madison chuckled. "*Not.* My mom got it from some movie friend of hers. Sometimes it's pretty convenient having a mom who has access to weird things like costume jewelry. You know?"

"Yeah, I guess. I don't really wear jewelry."

He laughed and Madison squirmed a little.

"Maddie!" Aimee skipped over toward them. "We have to dance to this song. Hart, get Egg and Drew to come dance."

Pretty soon, Aimee, Fiona, Madison, Hart, Egg, Chet, and Drew were out on the dance floor along with dozens of other Far Hills students. Everyone was twisting and shaking together.

It was one of those songs where everyone is supposed to do the same motions at the same time. During a slower part in the song, everyone sinks down, down, down to the floor and then jumps back up again.

Madison was bouncing in her caftan and waving her arms like before. She lifted the bottom of her dress up a little so she could move her legs more during the song's faster parts. It was hard doing everything at the same time, though. Right next to her, Hart moved up and down to the rhythm the best he could, too.

Madison could not believe that she was dancing right next to Hart Jones.

He was so cute!

After a while, the music slowed down and everyone started to sink toward the floor. Madison followed along, happy for the slowed-down pace. She listened close because she knew that in the next part of the song, everyone was supposed to get back up again.

Madison believed with all her heart that if she

jumped up at the perfect, timed moment, Hart would be impressed.

The music pumped a steady beat. Madison held her breath and then . . .

Jump!

She jumped up so fast—and didn't trip on the hem of her long caftan!

The only problem was that when she jumped, no one else did.

She stood there, upright, staring down at an ocean of costumed faces. Everyone stared back. Hart stared back. Three seconds went by.

It felt like slo-mo eternity.

Waaaaaaaaaaaaaaaaaah!

Some kid across the room screamed as he leaped into the air on the proper beat. Everyone was knocking around and shaking bodies upright again. Aimee spun in a few twirls.

Madison felt hot all over. She stopped dancing right then and there—and made a beeline for the punch with flies.

Ivy was standing there next to the drink table. "Like your costume, Madison," she said when Madison sped over, breathless.

Madison didn't believe her, of course. "Yeah—you too," Madison said.

"I made my costume, you know," Ivy bragged. "I figured that being a devil was fun, so I sewed this together." She was talking about the teeny skirt wrapped around her waist.

"Mmmm-uh-huh," Madison replied, taking a bite of a potato chip from the bowl next to her. She nibbled on the edge of the chip so it would last longer.

"You guys were all dancing as a group," Ivy said. "How cute."

Madison wanted to say, Didn't see you dancing, but instead she nodded and said, "Mmmm-uh-huh," again.

"This music really stinks, right?" Ivy complained. "Total disaster."

"Aren't you supposed to be a little more positive?" Madison asked. "Seeing as how you're our seventh-grade class president and all?"

Before Ivy could snap back with some clever answer, Aimee rushed up. "Where did you go?" she asked Madison. "I turned around and you vanished."

"I was thirsty. This costume is hot," Madison said.

"Later," Ivy said, snapping her gum. "I'm going to go dance." Ivy walked directly over toward the boys. Madison watched her stand next to Hart. She started talking to him, smiling and flipping her hair, leaning in because the music was loud. Hart didn't seem *that* interested, but Ivy kept pushing herself up against him. She turned around once and caught Madison's eye—and smiled.

Madison never knew a smile could feel like a punch in the gut.

Eventually the music died down a little and a

slower song came on. Madison figured at that point, Hart would stop dancing altogether. Maybe, in the utterly fantastic world of her imagination, Hart would ask *Madison* to dance.

But he didn't do either of those things. He danced with *Ivy*.

Madison's eyes were on them as they rocked back and forth to a pop song that she didn't like one bit.

"Check them out," Chet said, motioning to the dance floor. He was looking for a drink at the table.

Madison just shook her head, not looking. She didn't want to see any more.

"I can't believe they're dancing together," Chet said. "I really didn't know Egg liked my sister."

"Your sister? Wha?" Madison looked up and did a double take.

It wasn't Hart and Ivy Chet was watching. Egg and Fiona were the ones dancing together. Egg even had one of Fiona's leis around his neck. They weren't standing that close, but close enough so they were swaying back and forth to the same rhythm. Close enough to be holding hands, too, but Madison couldn't see if they were doing that.

Madison spun around to see if Hart and Ivy were dancing together. But they had disappeared. There was no wizard hat or her fire-red costume anywhere in the room. Aimee was also missing! Madison felt her pulse race.

"My wife tells me you're a whiz at computers,"

Dr. Wing said, walking right up to Madison. He had removed his wolf-doctor mask to get a drink of fruit punch.

"Oh," Madison said, startled to see him. Aimee was right. He was very cute.

"You help her with the Web site. That's hard work," Dr. Wing said.

"I guess." Madison caught herself staring with nothing to talk to him about. She fished for information. "What kind of doctor are you, Dr. Wing?"

He smiled. "I'm a wolf-doctor, remember?"

Madison chuckled. "No, really. What do you do for a job?"

"I'm serious!" he said. "Well, some people call me a veterinarian."

Madison gasped. Mrs. Wing's husband was a vet? She couldn't believe it. Madison had dozens . . . no, *hundreds* . . . of questions.

"I love animals!" Madison blurted.

"Well, me too." Dr. Wing smiled.

"I mean, I think I would be a good vet someday," Madison explained. "I don't know how you become one, but I love animals more than anything on the planet. Really and truly."

Dr. Wing grinned. He told Madison about an injured bird that had come to his office that morning. Just then, Poison Ivy fluttered by. She and her drones gave Madison a meaner-than-mean look.

"I have to go," Madison said abruptly, shaken by

the look. She wanted to find Fiona and Aimee. "Nice meeting you," Madison added.

Dr. Wing reached out to shake Madison's hand. "Anytime you want to, come around my office. We have a boarding, grooming, and pet adoption shelter attached to our building."

"Far Hills Animal Shelter? You're in charge of that place?" Madison said in disbelief. She knew exactly where he worked. It was where Aimee's family had adopted their basset hound, Blossom.

"Maddie!" Aimee came by again and grabbed Madison's wrist. "Sorry, Dr. Wing, I need her now."

"Aimee, did you know that Dr. Wing is a vet? Isn't that awesome? I just—"

"Come on!" Aimee pulled her over to a row of chairs and sat down.

"Let go of me." Madison rubbed her hand. "You're acting so weird."

"I saw Fiona and Egg dancing together," Aimee said.

"I saw them, too. Where were you, anyway? I was looking for you everywhere."

"Maddie! I was dancing with Egg and Fiona. That's why I'm so weirded out. We were goofing off together and then all of a sudden, Egg grabbed one of the leis off Fiona's neck."

"And . . . ?" Madison probed for more details. Had he held her hand? Grabbed her arm? Touched her head?

131

"I mean, for Egg to do that is like . . . a major *whoa*."

"It's just a dance, Aim," Madison said. "You said so yourself that a lot can happen here. You said our entire seventh-grade existence could be made by this dance. That's what you said."

"What does that have to do with Fiona and Egg?" Aimee asked.

"Maybe they like each other," Madison replied. She wanted to hear Fiona's side of the story before jumping to any conclusions.

"You're right, I guess," Aimee said, hanging her head. "I know you're right. It's just weird to me. Egg is like another brother, and I can't think of him that way."

"What way?" Madison said.

"Like a boy." Aimee shook her head.

"Everything's getting weird this year," Madison said.

Aimee lifted up her head. "Speak of the devil," she said, laughing, because Ivy really was dressed as a red devil tonight. "It's Miss Weird herself."

Poison Ivy walked right past Aimee and Madison and out the doors toward the bathrooms. Hart was right behind her.

"Hey, Finnster," Hart said.

"Hey, yourself. How—how's the dance going?" Madison asked, stuttering a little. She was so surprised to see him stop.

"Have you been in the scary hallway yet?" he asked them.

"Scary hallway? I went a little while ago," Aimee said. She'd gone in with some of her dance friends when Madison had been talking with Dr. Wing.

"You went, Aim? I haven't gone yet," Madison said. "Is it good?"

"I haven't gone, either! You wanna go with me?" Hart asked. "The line looks pretty short now."

Madison shrugged. "Okay. I guess."

Aimee didn't even suspect anything. She said she'd be fine with Fiona, Egg, Chet, and some other friends.

Madison and Hart went off to get on the line— alone. At least they were alone for five seconds.

That's when the red devil appeared—back from the bathroom already.

"Hey, Hart," Ivy said, talking right to him. "Oh, hello, Madison."

Hart was gearing up for some serious screaming inside the scary hallway. "Chet said overall it's kind of lame," he confessed. "But I say maybe it's fun to go through and try to scare the people who are already in there. Right?"

"We're gonna be scaring people?" Ivy asked.

Madison piped up. "Ivy, he just said that. . . ."

"Um, excuse me. If I needed a dictionary, I'd go to the library, thank you."

Madison bit her lip. "Like you *ever* go to the library," she said under her breath.

Hart turned to both girls and said, "This is so cool."

"I know," Ivy said, sliding up in line right next to him. They weren't holding hands or anything, but they were practically touching.

"Welcome to Scary Hallway!" a voice from behind a rubber mask croaked. Madison could tell it was Mr. Gibbons from the deep voice. "Aha!" he cried. "Look who we have here . . . more unwitting seventh graders to pass through the scary hallway . . . ha, ha, ha, ha!"

"Let's go, the line's moving," Ivy said to the kid who was standing in front of her, even though he was in another grade.

"You okay, Finnster?" Hart leaned back and whispered. "This looks pretty dorky now that we're actually here. I imagined something a lot different."

"I know what you mean," Madison said. She grinned and hoped in some secret way, underneath it all, he was talking about Ivy.

"C'mon!" Ivy said, yanking Hart inside, leaving Madison a step behind.

Madison growled to herself. They were gone. In a Halloween world, Madison was dealt the same thing every year: tricks after tireless tricks.

Chapter 13

"Eeeeeeeeeeeeek!" someone screamed in Madison's ear.

She screamed back even louder, almost keeling over in her Aphrodite dress.

Welcome to Scary Hallway.

Maneuvering in her caftan had been tough on the dance floor. It was even more difficult in this space. Plus it was hard to see where she was going. Madison felt so uncomfortable.

Up ahead of her, she heard Hart's whisper.

"You still there, Finnster?" he said.

"Yeah," Madison said. Where else would she be?

To her left, some kid with a rubber ax in his head leaned over and said, "Help me." He had fake blood oozing out of his mouth.

"Gross," Madison mumbled.

Another boy had one of those plastic fake hands that moved. "Here, let me give you a hand," he said, cackling. Madison laughed. The hand was one of the objects she and the other members of the committee had collected for the decorations. He must have lifted it off a table.

"Finnster!" Hart whispered again. "You there?"

"Yes!" she said again, but she really couldn't see anything now.

There were no scary people in her path for a few feet. Now the scary hallway was more like being blindfolded. Curtains folded in around her body as she walked farther along through the maze.

"Hart?" Madison whispered, coming to a sudden stop. She froze. Was someone there? She turned around but didn't see or hear anyone. "Hart?"

"Hart!" Ivy's voice boomed somewhere up ahead. "Don't go. Hold my hand!"

"I want to suck your blooooood!" Some girl with vampire fangs swooped over. She reached out and grabbed Madison's caftan.

"Don't touch me!" Madison screeched, stumbling backward. Now things were getting scarier.

Behind her somewhere, a group of kids started to scream. Not just little *eeeks* however. These were big, fat, *loud* screams—the kind to break an eardrum. They were just goofing around, but it was very annoying.

All of a sudden one of the kids inside the hallway was right up at Madison's back. He started to push. Madison was jostled.

"Move," the boy said.

Madison snapped, "I *can't* move."

When she said that, he pushed back a second time, much harder. "I said *move*," he yelled. Everyone was yelling. Madison felt hotter than hot.

She got her balance only to have him shove her a third time. And with that push, Madison went flying for real—dress, crown, scepter, and all.

Flying into Hart, that is. Much to her surprise, she had been jostled right over to the scary hallway exit.

Madison fell through the curtain opening and landed, hard. On top of Hart.

Hart got up first and then reached out to help Madison onto her feet. Taking his hand, Madison stood up, teetering. He had a warm, pink, sweaty hand, but she didn't mind. This was the hand she had hoped and prayed and crossed her fingers that she might hold at the dance.

Of course, the holding only lasted a split second. The moment Madison was back on two feet and Hart shook himself off, the hand was history. And not so long after that, the dance was history, too.

Fiona, Aimee, and Madison logged on to bigfish-bowl.com later that night so they could keep talking about the dance even after it was over. No one wanted the fun to end. They met up in a Friday night, private chat room called LYLAS, which meant "Love Ya Like a Sister."

```
<MadFinn>: I almost got stuck in
    SCARY hallway
<Wetwinz>: Some kid threw up in
    there I heard
<MadFinn>: No
<Wetwinz>: J/K
<BalletGrl>: So is Tommy getting
    expelled or what?
<MadFinn>: IDGI what's his prob?
    BOYS STINK!!!
<BalletGrl>: What's the deal with u
    and EGG, Fiona?
<Wetwinz>: :-)
<MadFinn>: It's cool if u like him
<BalletGrl>: I guess
<Wetwinz>: Can you believe who won
    the costume awards?
<Wetwinz>: That guy who was an
    eyeball in a tuxedo and got first
    was cool. He's in ninth grade.
<BalletGrl>: I liked the second-
    prize guy who dressed as all the
    characters from Scooby Doo.
<MadFinn>: Third place was funny.
    Bride of Frankenstein was cool.
<Wetwinz>: She was dancing with
    Frankenstein!
```

<Wetwinz>: Did you dance w/n e one
   Maddie
<BalletGrl>: No she didn't
<MadFinn>: Yes I did sorta
<Wetwinz>: WHO
<MadFinn>: No one 4get it!
<Wetwinz>: WHO????????
<BalletGrl>: I'm getting tired.
<Wetwinz>: LYLAS
<MadFinn>: LYLAS (2)
<BalletGrl>: I need a chat room
   dictionary!
<BalletGrl>: It's getting late
   almost 1030 whoa
<Wetwinz>: I have 2 go 2
<MadFinn>: Nooooo! stay
<BalletGrl>: Lets hang out
   tomorrow
<Wetwinz>: I have soccer
   remember?
<BalletGrl>: Oh yah
<MadFinn>: OH yah it's the
   CHAMPIONSHIPS!!!
<Wetwinz>: Yup I am PSYCHED
<MadFinn>: See u tomorrow
<Wetwinz>: *poof*
<BalletGrl>: Where did she go?
<MadFinn>: she logged off, aim.
<BalletGrl>: ok C U L8R bye
<MadFinn>: WAIT!!
<BalletGrl>: what

```
<MadFinn>: i have to tell you
   something ELSE
<BalletGrl>: what
<MadFinn>: Remember when we were
   @ my dad's & u saw that
   insta-message from someone named
   Bigwheels?
<BalletGrl>: No.
<MadFinn>: Oh.
<BalletGrl>: Huh?
<MadFinn>: well u did see an
   insta-message & the thing is that
   i did know who Bigwheels was.
   She's my keypal.
<BalletGrl>: Kewl
<MadFinn>: wait a minute u don't
   care?
<BalletGrl>: I wanna have online
   friends, too. Maybe I'll meet
   someone else who does ballet. U
   know?
<MadFinn>: u REALLY don't care?
   Really and truly?
<BalletGrl>: truly
<MadFinn>: Aim ur the best!!!
<BalletGrl>: C u at the game!
```

Madison said good-bye and logged off bigfish-bowl.com. She was a teeny bit disappointed that she hadn't won any of the costume prizes from the dance, but neither had Ivy. That was some consolation. Besides, what mattered most of all now was that she (1) had spent half the night with her crush (and her heart was happy), (2) spent major time with her BFFs, and (3) *finally* admitted the truth to Aimee about Bigwheels's existence.

Although it was very late after the chat, Madison still didn't feel tired. She stayed online and decided to write Bigwheels an e-mail.

She owed her one. So much had happened.

From: MadFinn
To: Bigwheels
Subject: Dances and Other News
Date: Fri 27 Oct 1:36 PM
Long time, no write.

Just got back fm. my school dance & I am blissed out.

I danced w/him. Yes, THE him I have been talking about since school started. He came dressed as a wizard. I had on this dumb costume. I went as a goddess.

Anyway, how r u? How r ur parents doing these days? I think about you whenever I see my mom & dad together. This is because my parents (u know this) are divorced. I think about your family.

How was your school dance? Write
back real soon.

XOXOXO Yours till the pumpkin pies,

MadFinn

P.S. Did you ever enter that
contest on bigfishbowl? I think
they will be sending winners
soon. I ended up liking my
story. Did you ever write that
poem?

After Madison sent the e-mail to her online friend, she finally changed into pajamas. After crawling out of Aphrodite's caftan, Madison combed the curls out of her hair, too. They were tangled where Mom had spritzed too much hair spray. She washed the blush off her face.

But she still wasn't so sleepy. Madison turned the computer back on.

 Scary

This past week in English, Mr. Gibbons
wrote on the board: Don't be afraid to
scare yourself. Half the class was like,
"WHAT??!"

He does that a lot, writes things we may
not understand. Asks us to talk. So it got
me thinking about a list of the things that

142

scare me. I thought of 8 so far.

What am I afraid of?

1. The dark
2. Failing
3. Being left out
4. Ghosts like Mrs. Martin
5. Really big zits
6. Dancing badly
7. Kissing a boy
8. Horror movies

Rude Awakening: Sometimes you have to dance the fright away! Amazingly, I tried dancing tonight. And even though my dress was too long, it worked. I felt less self-conscious and way less scared.

Am I gonna be scared of seventh grade forever???

I'M AFRAID NOT!

Ha ha ha.

Chapter 14

Saturday morning Madison woke up extra early so she could write in her files and clean up her room for real. She'd fake-cleaned it for Mom's benefit, but now the mess was beginning to grow and multiply once again.

Sweatpants and a training bra trailed out of the hamper.

Papers, files, and notebooks poked out from under the bed.

Even Madison's desk overflowed with magazines, schoolbooks, and two half-empty glasses of apple juice she forgot to bring back to the kitchen.

Madison checked her e-mailbox to see if she'd received any messages from bigfishbowl.com since last night. She was addicted to checking e-mails, especially when she was secretly hoping for a message back from Bigwheels *and* an update on the Caught in the Web contest. The results were supposed to have come in by now.

Her mailbox was flashing!

Madison grabbed at the edges of her desk and clicked the buttons to open her e-mailbox. Just as she'd hoped, there was a brand-new message from Bigwheels waiting there with a poem attachment.

From: Bigwheels
To: MadFinn
Subject: Re: Dances and Other News
Date: Sat 28 Oct 8:36 AM

I didn't make it to my school's
Halloween dance, but it sounds like
u had a great time. Congrats.
I am sitting here after school and
my mom just made me the yummiest
pumpkin cake. I am so happy cuz it
is my absolute favorite. Did you
decide to go trick-or-treating or
no? I think you said no but I can't
remember.

I wrote a poem BTW. Here you go
even if it is kinda silly. It was
for my class and I thought it might
make u laugh.

   Happy Halloween
   There once was a pumpkin on a farm

Who didn't like the other gourds.
The pumpkin reached one vine out
    like an arm
And spoke a few funny words.
"Halloween isn't fun without
    friends,"
the pumpkin said from his stem.
"My friends are all cut off down
    to the ends,"
And sure enough someone had
    picked them.
When you spend Halloween carving
    one
Remember what some pumpkins say,
Be with your friends and have fun
On a special Halloween day!!!

They haven't posted the winners yet
4 that contest. How did you do? I
bet you won it. FC!!! (That's
fingers crossed). I have this
feeling. N e way, write back soon.

Yours till the wind blows,

Bigwheels

Madison was becoming more and more convinced that Bigwheels was *her* twin—not like Fiona
and Chet—but close.

As she shut down the Bigwheels message,

Madison noticed her mailbox indicator flashing again. There was another message—and this one was from the bigfishbowl.com Web site! Madison held her breath and opened the document.

She read it aloud slowly to Phinnie, even though he wasn't paying much attention. He'd recurled up into a furry ball at her feet.

From: webmaster@bigfishbowl.com
To: Members Only
Subject: Caught in the Web Contest
Winners
Date: Sat 28 Oct 8:34 AM

Happy Halloween!

The big fins at bigfishbowl.com
asked YOU to write us a mystery
for Halloween. Your stories were
FRIGHTFULLY good. We received
over three hundred entries.
Thanks to everyone who wrote
stories!

The stories below will be posted
in their entirety starting on
HALLOWEEN.

Thanks for entering! And
congratulations to the winners.

And here's the top winners' list:

GRAND PRIZE: Blood and More, by QuakeKing21
RUNNERS-UP: Bat Breath, by PcenloveXO
Revenge of the Slugs, by LoriGirl
The Slayer, by Mariohottie
The Secret of the Old Trunk, by MadFinn

"I can't believe it!" Madison shouted when she saw her name on the screen. "Mom! Mom! I won! Come here!"

"Rowrooooo!" Phin awoke with a howl. *"Rowrooooo!"*

Madison had been selected as a runner-up. Phinnie barked his approval and jumped up for scritches on his back. Mom, hearing the racket, came into the bedroom to see what all the fuss was about.

"You won?" she cried.

"Well, I got a runner-up prize," Madison said, pulling Phinnie into her lap.

"Honey bear, that's fantastic!" Mom said sweetly, and patted Madison on the head. "We have to celebrate! Right now. Oh, I'm so proud of you, Maddie."

Madison felt all tingly inside. She was proud of herself, too. Although the Ivy drama had momentarily threatened to ruin seventh grade and the school dance for her, Madison was finding out that she could still have a very happy Halloween. Madison and Phinnie followed Mom into the kitchen, where she warmed up a special loaf of the pumpkin bread Madison loved.

"This is just turning into the best Halloween ever," Madison said, pouring herself a bowl of Lightly Honeyed Oaty-Os, too. Phin curled up by the dishwasher.

"Why is that, Maddie?" Mom buttered the slices of pumpkin bread.

"It just is." Madison took one bite and smiled.

Madison leaned over to feed Phin a corner of the pumpkin bread. He licked his chops for more.

"You know, I never won anything before, Mom," she said. "And I feel so happy right now. I really can't explain what I'm feeling."

Mom smiled. "It won't be the last time you win something, I promise you that."

Madison thanked Mom and went back upstairs to get dressed. She tried calling Aimee to tell her about the contest, but the Gillespie phone lines were busy. One of Aimee's brothers was always hogging the phone. She'd tell Aimee and everyone else about it later when they met up at the school soccer game.

Today was the *big* game everyone had been waiting for. The Rangers were up against the other most winning team in the district, the Cobras. The game was being hosted at Far Hills Junior High.

Aimee was going to the game straight from a private ballet lesson in the morning, so Madison walked to school by herself. As she crossed the parking lot and headed around back to the field,

Madison glanced at purple-and-orange posters taped to the doors of the school building.

Something to Scream About!

She laughed. The whole week had been a scream. A little piece of her wished she could be back at the dance again.

"Maddie!" Drew was running to the soccer field, too.

"Hey!" Madison said. "I just found out I won a writing Web contest. Well, I got runner-up."

"Congratulations," Drew said.

They walked over to the bleachers. Egg was sitting there, goofing around with Chet and another friend, Dan. Egg's sister, Mariah, was sitting there, too, with some of her older friends in black, the same ones Madison had seen at the mall food court the weekend before.

The stands were filling quickly with seventh, eighth, and ninth graders. Parents held up painted signs that read GO RANGERS! Everyone had on jackets and scarves to keep the wind away. The air was crisp, and smelled like leaves.

One side of the bleachers seemed to hold mostly Cobra fans, but no one was arguing or anything about which team was better—*yet*. Madison felt overwhelmed by the color, noise, and feelings in the pit of her stomach.

She really belonged. This was her school.

Mr. and Mrs. Waters were sitting down in front, sipping cups of coffee. Fiona, tying her laces, had her knee up on the bottom step of the bleachers. When she turned and saw Madison come across the field, she broke into a giant grin. "Maddie! You're here! That is so great!"

Fiona threw her arms around her friend. Madison hugged right back.

"Where's Aimee?" Fiona asked. Then she remembered about the ballet lesson. Aimee would be coming later, close to the first whistle.

"So I gotta go," Fiona blurted. "Thanks for coming! See you after the game!" She hugged Madison one last time and then ran over to her team's huddle for warm-ups and pep talks.

"Hey, Maddie," Mariah said, waving. She turned to the guy on her left and said, "This is Karl." Karl nodded in Madison's direction.

"Hey, howyadoing?" he said. She smiled and wondered if maybe he was cuter than she and Aimee and Fiona first thought at the mall.

"So how was the Halloween dance?" Mariah asked Madison discreetly.

"Fine. I went as Aphrodite," Madison whispered back.

"Ooooh," Mariah teased. "Goddess of love!" Luckily no one but Karl heard her say that. He didn't seem to care about anything they said.

"I didn't see you there," Madison said.

Mariah shrugged. "Nah, I blew it off. Karl and I went to the movies. But I'm glad you had a nice time. I bet you looked good."

Madison lowered her head, a little embarrassed. She turned to watch Fiona take practice kicks out on the field.

"Where's Hart?" Chet asked Egg. Madison turned to hear the answer.

"He is way sick," Drew replied. Since he and Hart were cousins, their mothers had spoken that morning.

"Sick?" Madison said.

"*Way* sick. Like throwing up."

"Ewwww, gross me," Egg said. "Maybe he ate the flies in that punch last night."

Drew and Chet both snorted.

"So I guess he's not coming to the game, then?" Madison asked.

"There's Aimee!" Chet cried. "She looks like Barney!"

Aimee was running up the side of the field with a purple duffel bag. She had on a purple sweatshirt and leggings, too.

Madison stood up so Aimee would see where they were sitting.

"Hiya, everyone!" Aimee said, sitting down on the edge of the bleachers. "I am so wiped out. We had a guest at our ballet lesson this morning. We had to do these exercises over and over—"

"Yeah, Aimee, like we care about your ballet lesson," Egg cracked.

"Egg!" Madison cracked back. "And like we care about anything you have to say, either."

"Thanks, Maddie." Aimee smiled.

"That's cool that you take private lessons," Chet said. Drew agreed.

Aimee smiled back at them. She sneered at Egg.

"May I have your attention, please!" someone yelled from the soccer field. It was one of the referees speaking into a portable loudspeaker system. *"Your attention, please!"*

"Go, Cobras!" someone on the other side of the bleachers screeched.

"Welcome to the Far Hills district championship."

Madison scanned the playing field for Fiona. She was jogging in place, chatting with teammates, eating an orange. She was getting set to win. Madison knew that this would be a special day in the history of the seventh grade.

"Say cheese!" Mrs. Waters said, pointing a camera up toward the bleachers. She snapped a photo of Egg, Chet, Drew, Dan, Madison, Aimee, Mariah, Karl, and whoever else could squeeze into the photo.

"Now, let us introduce our teams!"

"Rangers *rule*!" a group of girls yelled out a few rows behind Madison and her friends. Everyone cheered.

When Fiona came out onto the field, the

153

applause soared. Madison clapped as hard as she possibly could. Aimee was screaming at the top of her lungs. Chet, Drew, and Egg were yelling, "Woo woo," like dogs.

"Rangers rock! Rangers shake! Go, Fiona! No more snake!" Madison and Aimee had planned a special cheer in Fiona's honor.

"That's pretty good, Maddie," Egg said.

Madison grinned.

"And don't forget we want everyone to play fair!" the loudspeaker voice boomed. A coach recited rules from the junior high school soccer bible. Strict rules about sportsmanship needed to be followed down on the field. While the rules were being read, Fiona stuck her arm up and waved to everyone in the stands. Mrs. Waters snapped more pictures.

"Go, Fiona!" Aimee and Madison yelled at the same time. They cheered so much throughout the game. They were hoarse at the end.

With two minutes left in the game, the score was tied 3–3. A halfback kicked the ball over to Fiona at the right wing position. She took off down the field.

"Go! Go! Go!"

It sounded like everyone in the stands was cheering at the same time, even Karl.

No one was following her down the field. The goalie appeared panicked, jumping from foot to foot, side to side.

"She's gonna make a goal, I know it!" Aimee screeched.

"Go, Fiona!" Chet called out.

Fiona got within yards of the goal, and it looked like she was going to make a kick in, when all of a sudden she surprised everyone.

She kicked the ball to the side. She passed it to one of her teammates, Daisy Espinoza

And Daisy kicked it right in.

"Score!"

The Cobra goalie didn't know what happened until it was too late.

"We won!" Aimee yelled right in Madison's ear. They were jumping up and down and the bleachers were shaking. Aimee threw her arms around Madison.

Down on the field, Fiona and Daisy ran over to each other, arms in the air. They embraced. Madison felt a surge of excitement. The rest of the team ran up, too, and slapped Fiona on the back.

"My sister rocks!" Chet said. He dropped his cool exterior for two seconds to bask in Fiona's soccer skills. The fact that Fiona was a star on the team only made everything else that much sweeter for Madison and her friends.

Madison smiled to herself. The only ghosts in Far Hills now were fading memories of elementary school.

Seventh grade had many more treats in store. Madison could feel it in her Halloween bones.

Mad Chat Words:

9	Yummy
<:-	Stupid question
;-]	Smirking
EMSG	E-mail message
F2F	Face-to-face
BF	Best friend or Boyfriend
FC	Fingers crossed
<ggg>	Grin
LYLAS	Love ya like a sister
LYLAS (2)	Love ya like a sister x 2/twice
4get it	Forget it
Cuz	Because
N e way	Anyway

<u>Madison's Computer Tip:</u>

I've been getting weird e-mails from people I don't know. Egg and Drew told me that sometimes strangers send viruses and gross stuff over the Internet. You could download something bad onto your computer and not even realize it. **Never download files from unknown senders.** Even if I'm really, really curious, I always ask my parents first or I just delete it.

Visit Madison at www.madisonfinn.com

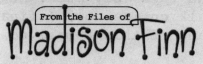
Chapter 1

"Nooooooo!" Madison covered her face with her hands and peeked through her fingers.

This e-mail was bad news.

From: GoGramma
To: MadFinn
Subject: Thanksgiving
Date: Sat 11 Nov 7:56 AM

I am so very sorry, Maddie, but I won't be coming to your house for Thanksgiving. My hip problem is back and I'm not traveling anywhere. Your aunt Angie is spending the holiday with your uncle Bob's family, so our traditional visit is on hold until next year. Don't be sad. I will miss you and Phin very much. At least we can talk online now. I finally have the hang of this e-mail now.

How did your report card go? How is your friend Aimee? Write me another letter.

Love, Gramma

Madison groaned as she reread the message for the third time. When Gramma Helen didn't like something, she would say, "Maddie, that is for the birds." That was exactly how Madison felt right now. Only this Thanksgiving was going to be "for the turkeys."

How could Gramma not come to Far Hills? Madison deleted the yucky message.

For the past twelve years, Madison's parents had hosted a major feast every Thanksgiving. Mom's mom, Gramma Helen, and Mom's sister, Aunt Angie, and her husband, Uncle Bob, would travel on the plane from Chicago to New York. Dad's brother, Uncle Rick, would even come from Canada with his wife, Violet, even though Canadians celebrate their Thanksgiving in October.

The Finn house had been the epicenter of everyone's Thanksgiving universe for as long as Madison could remember.

Mom always decorated the house with paper

turkeys and gourds and pumpkins and spice candles. All of the town guests slept on sleeper sofas around the house—except for Gramma. Madison gave up her bedroom for Gramma. But she didn't mind. Madison loved having the house full of people . . . and so did Phin. He loved all the extra attention.

Thanksgiving morning meant sleeping in, watching the Macy's parade on TV, and eating way too much good food. Dad wore an extra-large poofy white hat and called himself the house super-chef. Madison was his unofficial chef-ette. She got up at five in the morning to help him make the best cornbread stuffing on the planet.

But not this year.

This year Dad wouldn't be in the Finn kitchen thanks to the big D—D for divorce. And thanks to Gramma's bad hip and Aunt Angela and Uncle Bob's changed plans, there would be no out-of-town visitors. There wouldn't even be turkey on Madison's dinner table. Unfortunately, Mom was a vegetarian who wanted to save the turkeys, not baste them.

Madison had visions of eating a Thanksgiving bean burrito and tofu stuffing with cranberry sauce this year.

Phin was curled up in a ball on the floor, snoring, oblivious to the change in holiday plans. Would he miss the Thanksgiving attention even more than Madison would? He'd surely miss turkey scraps tossed under the table.

3

"Maddie, did you call me? Do you need something?" Mom rushed upstairs and found Madison curled up on her plastic purple chair in the center of her room. "I heard you scream and . . . hey! What's that look on your face?"

Madison pouted. "Gramma can't come to Thanksgiving." She leaned over to pet Phin's ears. He made a snuffling noise.

"She e-mailed you, huh?" Mom frowned. "She said she would."

Madison could tell from Mom's tone of voice that she knew about the change in plans already.

"I'm sorry, honey bear," Mom added. "Gramma wanted to tell you herself. I know how disappointed you must—"

"Thanksgiving *stinks*." Madison crossed her arms. "Can't we go to Chicago to see everyone?"

"I told you I have work commitments that week. I'm so sorry, Maddie. Really I am. Next year we can—"

"Next year?" Madison said. "What about this year?"

"This year will be just the two of us. Is that so bad?" Mom chuckled, trying to make light of the situation. But Madison wasn't laughing back.

"I knew everything would be ruined when I saw a black cat yesterday," Madison moaned. She believed that it was terrible luck for a person to walk under ladders or cross a black cat's path. Bad

Thanksgiving luck had definitely found her.

"But we'll have fun together!" Mom said with a big smile. "Won't we?"

"I guess," Madison shrugged.

Mom took a deep breath.

"What's Aimee doing for Thanksgiving?"

"Having a normal day. Her family isn't divorced," Madison snapped.

The moment she'd said the words, Madison knew how hurtful they sounded. She reached for Mom's arm.

"I didn't mean that," Madison gulped. "I am so sorry, Mom."

Mom threw her arms around Madison's shoulders and squeezed. "I'm sorry, too. I know our new arrangement takes some getting used to. But Angie and Bob will come next year. So will Gramma."

As Mom hugged, Madison felt all her feelings swell up inside like she would burst. But she held back from crying.

"Let's just make the best of it, okay, Maddie?" Mom said, gently smoothing the top of Madison's head.

Madison nodded. She didn't really have a choice. Whether she liked it or not, certain rules about holidays had been set up in the Finns' divorce arrangement. The judge had ruled that Mom and Dad swapped Madison from holiday to holiday. This year, Mom got Thanksgiving. Next year, Dad would.

The back-and-forth between Mom and Dad made Madison dizzier than dizzy on a regular basis. Holidays, however, were proving to be the worst. In this family tug-of-war, Madison Finn was *definitely* all pulled out.

The doorbell zinged. Madison leaped up and dashed downstairs to get the door.

Aimee was standing on the back porch, arms waving in the air, her dog Blossom's tail thwacking against the sliding doors. From inside, Phin started panting. He was so happy to see his doggy girlfriend through the glass.

"What are you doing here, Aim? I was just gonna call you!" Madison said as she opened the doors. Blossom dashed inside and ran off with Phin.

Aimee struck a pose with her hands up in the air. She was wearing a brand-new yellow winter parka.

"Whaddya think?" she asked. "I ordered it online from Boop-Dee-Doop. Well, my mother did. We ordered it on her credit card. My first Internet purchase ever. . . ."

Madison shook her head. "Cool color."

"It's called 'Lemon Drop,'" Aimee said.

"It's nice. But in case you hadn't noticed, Aimee, it's like fifty degrees outside."

Aimee pulled the jacket off. "I know. I know. But I just couldn't wait to show you. That's why I came over."

Madison decided to make it a special occasion.

She took out the blender to make yellow fruit smoothies in honor of the jacket. Making smoothies was one of Madison's favorite things to do.

"Put extra banana in mine," Aimee asked.

They watched the blender go.

"I just found out my gramma isn't coming for Thankgiving," Madison said, adding ice into the machine.

"Bummer," Aimee sighed.

"Yeah," Madison sighed back. She poured the smoothie into a glass. "So what is happening at your house for the holiday?"

Aimee shrugged and took a big slurp. "Mom is making some kind of health food dinner, as usual. My brothers begged for turkey, so we're having one of those, too. You know the drill."

"Uh-huh. The drill."

Aimee looked at Madison sideways. "Is something wrong, Maddie?"

"I wish that I had the usual drill for Thanksgiving."

"Yeah, you have to spend Thanksgiving without your dad," Aimee said. "That's stinky."

"Without my dad. Without my gramma," Madison said. "Without *everyone*. It's just gonna be Mom and me. And two people can't have a real Thanksgiving alone together."

"Why don't you guys go to Chicago?" Aimee asked.

"Mom's work." Madison sighed. "Some project she has to do. I wish I were you or Fiona. She gets to go all the way to California for Thanksgiving."

Fiona Waters was Madison and Aimee's brand new seventh-grade best friend. She'd moved to Far Hills from California over the summer with her twin brother, Chet.

"Fiona said her gramps has a great big swimming pool out there," Aimee giggled. "They'll be swimming on Thanksgiving! Now *that's* weird."

Aimee stood up and twirled around. She danced when she wanted to cheer her friends up, and Madison looked like she could use some cheering.

Madison cracked a smile.

"So are you gonna do that extra-credit project in social studies?" Aimee asked, waving her arms in a circle over her head.

Social studies was the one class Madison, Aimee, and Fiona had together. Their teacher, Miss Belden, had a reputation for being one of the toughest teachers in junior high—but she always gave kids a chance to do extra-credit projects. She said hard work was good, but it was just as important to have fun.

"I don't get why she calls it extra credit when *everyone* has to do it," Madison moaned. "And why do we all have to pair up?"

"I don't know. But we could do our project together. We can make a turkey or something."

"A turkey?" Madison exclaimed. "Like what? A turkey sandwich?"

Aimee laughed. "Sure. Let's make a mini-replica of the first Thanksgiving dinner with little drumsticks and corn on the cobs . . ."

"Hey, what time is it?" Madison asked all of a sudden.

Outside the sun was dipping down in the sky. It cast the entire room in an orange glow.

Aimee looked at her yellow wristwatch. She had watchbands to color-coordinate with each outfit, including her new parka. "Wow, it's almost five o'clock. Already four-thirty."

"It's getting late. Let's take the dogs out," Madison squealed. "Blossom! BLOSSOM!"

Phin and Blossom came running. They were panting like crazy.

"Wanna go OUT?" Madison said. Aimee laughed and grabbed the leashes.

It was fun to walk the dogs together. Madison and Aimee liked to think that their dogs were best friends, just like them.

When Madison returned home, Mom was perched on the sofa watching edited reels from one of her documentary films.

"I'm going up to my room," Madison announced. Mom didn't flinch.

"I'm going up to my room," Madison announced again, louder this time.

"Okay. Dinner's in an hour," Mom said, waving her off. "And clean that mess. And finish your homework."

Madison made a face, only Mom didn't see it. Mom sounded like a recorded message: *Do this. Clean that.*

Once upstairs, Madison consciously decided not to pick *anything* up. She crawled over her enormous pile of clothes and pile of files and collapsed into her purple chair. There were much better things to do than clean her room! She powered up her laptop.

Madison had only intended to log on, send an e-mail back to Gramma, and log off. But once online, she got *way* distracted from those tasks. She surfed around and went to the home page for bigfish-bowl.com. There was a new feature advertised on a flashing yellow banner across the top.

Just Fishing Around! The Ultimate Search Engine!

Madison typed in the word DOG for fun, just to see what a search on her favorite subject might turn up. Madison was pleasantly surprised to see 3,412 possible matches and started reading. Links were underlined.

```
Dog Owner's Guide: Welcome to Dog
Owner's Guide
```
If you have a dog, want a dog, or love dogs, you've come to the right place for all kinds of information about living with and loving dogs.

Includes Dog Screen Saver, more.

<u>Dog Emporium Online</u>
Flea collars, heartworm pills, soft
beds, chew toys, rawhide . . .
everything discounted for your
family dog.

<u>Dog of the Day—Sign Yours Up Now</u>
Tell us about your special dog. Is
your bischon frise funny? Does your
weimaraner whine? Winners daily!

Madison added a few more words to the search
to find dog links closer to home. She typed in DOG,
FAR HILLS, NEW YORK—separated by the required
commas. A familiar name popped up.

Madison knew this vet!

<u>Far Hills Animal Shelter, Clinic,
Dog Boarding</u>
Welcome from Bryan Wing, DVM, and
staff. Full service, referrals, dog
boarding, tales of homeless pets,
breed tips, dog grooming care.
Volunteers needed!

Dr. Wing was married to Madison's computer
teacher, Mrs. Wing. This was the direct link for Dr.
Wing's Web site.

On the site's home page there was a photograph

of a basset hound that looked just like Aimee's dog, Blossom. That dissolved slowly into a photo of a yellow Labrador retriever (who was really more cream-colored than yellow), and a teeny dachshund named Rosebud. More flashing type at the bottom of the screen read: *Come and visit our offices!* There was a teeny photograph of Dr. Wing and a short letter underneath that.

Welcome to Far Hills Animal Shelter and Clinic! We're glad you've stopped into the section of our "virtual" animal shelter. For ten years, my team has been dedicated to pet rescue and care in Far Hills. Working with shelters, veterinarians, and other concerned businesses, we hope to eliminate our homeless pet problem and care for sick and abandoned animals in our area. Won't you please become a volunteer and help out?

"Rooooowowf!" Phin barked. He was curled up into a ball by the base of Madison's purple chair. Madison scritched Phin's head.

The idea of helping out at the animal shelter seemed so exciting. Maybe this year's Thanksgiving didn't have to be for the turkeys after all? Maybe this Thanksgiving could be for the *dogs* instead?

Phin would *definitely* love that.

12